MEN WHO WALK IN DREAMS

GUERNICA WORLD EDITIONS 80

MEN WHO WALK IN DREAMS

MARISA LABOZZETTA

GUERNICA
World
EDITIONS

TORONTO–CHICAGO–BUFFALO–LANCASTER (U.K.)
2024

Guernica Editions Founder: Antonio D'Alfonso

Michael Mirolla, general editor
Jennifer Dinsmore, editor
Cover design: Allen Jomoc, Jr.
Interior design: Jill Ronsley, suneditwrite.com
Front cover image: Shirley and John Piniat

Guernica Editions Inc.
1241 Marble Rock Rd., Gananoque (ON), Canada K7G 2V4
2250 Military Road, Tonawanda, N.Y. 14150-6000 U.S.A.
www.guernicaeditions.com

Distributors:
Independent Publishers Group (IPG)
600 North Pulaski Road, Chicago IL 60624
University of Toronto Press Distribution (UTP)
5201 Dufferin Street, Toronto (ON), Canada M3H 5T8

First edition.

Legal Deposit—Third Quarter
Library of Congress Catalog Card Number: 2024931772
Library and Archives Canada Cataloguing in Publication
Title: Men who walk in dreams / Marisa Labozzetta.
Names: Labozzetta, Marisa, author.
Series: Guernica world editions (Series) ; 80.
Description: First edition. | Series statement: Guernica world editions ; 80 |
Short stories.
Identifiers: Canadiana (print) 20240307704 | Canadiana (ebook)
20240307712 | ISBN 9781771839075 (softcover) |
ISBN 9781771839082 (EPUB)
Subjects: LCGFT: Short stories.
Classification: LCC PS3562.A2356 M46 2024 | DDC 813/.54—dc23

For
Ethan, Luke, Jason, and Jacoby
The little men who stand tall in my life

What is life? a tale that is told;
What is life? a frenzy extreme,
A shadow of things that seem;
And the greatest good is but small,
That all life is a dream to all,
And that dreams themselves are a dream.

—**Pedro Calderón de la Barca,**
Life is a Dream (La vida es sueño),
translated from the Spanish

Contents

Men Who Walk in Dreams 1

The Woman Who Drew on Walls 18

For the Love of Buffaloes 33

The Sound of Your Voice 61

The Intruder 83

Amnesia 93

You Can't Get There from Here 108

Holway Street 120

Cocullo 138

Sunrise 151

Acknowledgments 171

About the Author 172

Men Who Walk in Dreams

I was born late—several weeks, a month maybe. At least that's what my mother always told me. Of course she had no real way of knowing, since my father's evenings included several glasses of wine and carnal demands that kept her barely menstruating for more than twenty years. "Stubborn," my mother said. "The worst time with you. Always the worst." I reveled in the superlative from the very beginning: when you are deemed the worst from conception, your possibilities are limitless and your desires, no matter how destructive, never unrealistic. That's why when Salvatore—Father Nania—rode his donkey up the hill and into our sleepy town of Fossato Serralta, I knew he was within my reach.

Like the female counterpart to my father, I emerged into this world with an appetite: the gnawing between my legs made itself apparent before I could speak its name, and the actions I took to quell it were but a natural consequence. At nine years of age, my eyes met those of the towering young vicar ten years my senior with clarity of intent: I knelt before him—the carved wooden altar rail our only barricade—and interpreted the Latin words he uttered as we both crossed ourselves to be a confirmation of mutual understanding. "I will wait for you," they said. "Amen."

With no more than a pat on the head, the perfunctory kiss on both cheeks, the slight caress with his finger whenever he gripped my hand, the years passed as Father Nania ate at our table and those of other townspeople whenever he returned from neighboring villages to his ministry in Fossato Serralta. He occasionally appeared in my dreams, but mostly other men surfaced, often familiar strangers whose faces I knew but strained without success to place. They serenaded me beneath the narrow, iron-grated balcony of our stone house, where my father wove baskets for dried fruit that was exported to America. Sometimes they merely walked by, casting no more than a glance in my direction. However they appeared, all left me straining to identify them. Men who still resided in Fossato Serralta? Men from my short-lived past? From another life entirely, or maybe a future one? Or perhaps they had returned from a former dream and were just that: the men who walked in dreams only.

When I turned sixteen, I knelt before Father Nania as I had many times before and prepared to make my confession—not of missed Masses or disobedience to my parents, but of what he already knew: I was in love with him. After a long silence, he told me to meet him in the sacristy when he had finished listening to the other parishioners who sought absolution. Then, blessing me for the last time, he shut the tiny door of the confessional and, with equal determination, on the priesthood, forever.

* * *

Despite his imposing frame, I knew that to most men Salvatore appeared slight because of his gentle—almost timid—ways. His reserve would only increase after we arrived in America due to his attempt to keep a low profile. Regardless of how he had acquired the trait, he would use it to keep his family's life in the shadows because, in the eyes of the Catholic Church, he remained a priest. Why, he had officiated at his own marriage—our marriage—witnessed only by the moon and the stars of a late-summer sky.

Our disgraced flight to America seemed no more singular than that of any other young couple when we boarded at the Bay of Naples. We had arrived late because Salvatore's donkey that carried us, with our few possessions, had died along the way, forcing us to walk the last part. Therefore we missed the ship that sailed for Buenos Aires and waited days, sleeping on the windy shore, sharing our bread and ham with strangers, until we all boarded a vessel headed for New York. Buenos Aires was farther away from Italy, farther from our scandal than America, and maybe the accommodations on a ship heading in that direction would also have been different. All of it a misunderstanding: ships, we later learned, never sailed to Buenos Aires from Naples unless the steamship company was paid a handsome incentive and the ship changed course midstream; and steerage always meant assignment to the noisy, fuel-smelling bowels of the vessel by the rudder. But we were ignorant of so many things.

"Drink, *caru. È bonu.* Sip," Salvatore said, pleading, each day we were on board. The large hand he had used to place the sacred host on the tongues of my family now held out a spoonful of broth he tried to convince me was good, steadied my forehead, and cleaned the product of retching so violent I feared it would contain the dispelled beginnings of my child. My earliest resentment of him surfaced briefly then because of his ability to spend small amounts of time up on the open deck, while I proved to be the weaker one who suffered without letup from seasickness exacerbated by the nausea of early pregnancy. October 19, 1922, marked the end of the two-week voyage. I disembarked from the *Conte Rosso*, which had not been persuaded to sail to South America, ten pounds lighter.

* * *

A *patrone* could smell desperation, and we innocently wore it like a flapping banner when we finally disembarked from the ferry that took us from the steamship to the crowded, bustling pavements of New York City. What good fortune we believed we had been blessed with! A distinguished-looking man in a tan tweed suit, starched white shirt, red-and-tan striped tie, and flat-top felt hat not only spoke our Calabrese but knew of a farm high on a hill that was in need of a caretaker: a furnished house, fifteen acres of land bordered by tall pines to do with as we pleased, a small salary that seemed like a windfall, and all with the sole obligation of raising turkeys.

A secluded place far removed from the city and any *paesani* we might one day encounter who were privy to "our sin," as Salvatore called it. "God has provided," he said, brushing my pale cheek.

The man, not much older than Salvatore, handed us five ten-dollar bills, the address of a Mr. Martin who would take us to our new home from the station, and train fare. *Madonna!* This was truly the Promised Land, Salvatore said, and we were the chosen— the forgiven, he found it necessary to add, while I saw no need for forgiveness. The five additional dollars to vote Republican when we were naturalized we accepted without question. Had there been an alternative? Choice was not our luxury.

Mr. Martin did not speak Italian. No one in the town of Millers Falls did. Not the Thompsons, who owned the dairy farm, or Mr. O'Reilly at the post office. No one. Their families had immigrated decades earlier, though at the time I believed they had been in Millers Falls from America's beginning. There was a small stone church, much like the one in Fossato Serralta, in the center of town, but to Salvatore's relief it was not a Catholic one to remind him of his abandoned calling. Mr. Martin held the keys to the small white stucco house with light-green concrete steps. He carried a large metal crate of flour, cornmeal, rice, salt, pepper, and coffee from his dry goods store, along with some apples and wilted greens— enough to carry us through several weeks—through a screen door and then a heavier wooden one, painted green to match the steps. Eggs, he said, would be delivered weekly by the landlord, and milk—which we never drank—could be picked up by Salvatore from the Thompsons' dairy farm on the days he took the horse and wagon to town.

The landlord came to Millers Falls only one or two days a week, when he and his son tended to the chickens they raised at the foot of the southern side of the hill in a sizable barn whose roof was barely visible from the parcel of land we were to live and work on. We were never to venture down that side of the hill. All this we learned from Adela, the interpreter who accompanied him. Her family had immigrated to America from Bari when she was only two years old, and while her dialect was at times difficult to understand, we were relieved yet at the same time fearful: her town was nearly four hundred kilometers from Fossato Serralta, but still, could it have been possible for her relatives to have received word about us? Was this all some kind of *ingannu*—a trick to punish us? Imprison us? Adela, however, seemed unaware of our circumstance, and so we trusted her to tell us the truth. What else were we to do?

"She looks a little like a starving goat," Salvatore said of Adela after we had been left to settle into our new home.

"That's because she has no neck and a pointed chin."

"Ah, you're right!"

"And she's small and round and a little hunched."

"*Che peccatu!*" Salvatore said, shaking his head.

"She seems happy enough. Save your pity for us. Save your eyes and thoughts for me, *caru miu*," I said. I pressed my body against his to keep warm during the chilly autumn night in our first real bed, knowing his body was never cold, and he was eager to remove my nightgown, to feel my cool flesh, to make love. We were a good fit: *I* overflowing with the cravings and curiosities he had denied himself to even acknowledge.

"How was it possible?" he often asked, whispering, so drunk with lust as his enormous frame swam in the waters of my petite body that sometimes I thought he would crush me. "How could I have ever thought I could live without this—you? *T'amu*," he said, professing his love.

"Am I still desirable?" I asked, aware of the effects of our grueling voyage, and the belly that had begun to swell, though I already knew the answer.

He lifted his head for a moment, just to smile and as though to say, "Watch how much I desire you." Then he sucked on my engorged breasts and buried his face places that made me dig my nails into his skin. Just as a priest ends his daily noontime breviary with a chanted Amen, Salvatore concluded his sexual ritual with a loud utterance of satisfaction and gratitude not just to me, but, oddly enough, to God.

* * *

In contrast to the houses in my village, our new home sprawled because it was all—except for the attic and cellar—on one floor: a kitchen with a wood-burning oven and stovetop; a bathroom with sink, tub, and toilet; and three more rooms—one with a brick fireplace. The doorframes were low, and I reminded Salvatore to stand tall when he passed from room to room, fearing that his constant ducking would eventually leave him with a stooped posture like Adela's. After all, it had been his height that had attracted me to him more than his looks, which were similar to those of other men in town: dark hair and eyes, bushy brows, full nose and lips, olive complexion. But the men in my village were not much taller than me. Salvatore towered above them all like the cathedral's spire in our provincial capital of Catanzaro, where it was said women flocked to Mass just to observe the big hands up close when he administered Communion, or, better yet, touched their heads as he innocently bestowed blessings while they fantasized about the size of his most private part. His unavailability made his shy personality a magnet to which women clung and a source of jealousy that men belittled.

The day after our arrival, Salvatore found an axe in the toolshed and took it to the trunk and branches of a small fallen oak tree near the pump house of an artesian well that we'd first mistook for a miniature outhouse. He stacked a good pile of the split logs in the kitchen next to the stove. Before lunch, he was already working on a cradle for the baby while I climbed the narrow attic steps—so vertical I had to hang on to the banister to keep my balance. Had Salvatore known what I was doing, especially in my condition, he would have called me down, or at least tried, and he would have received a lesson regarding my obstinacy. The attic's slanted ceiling was far too low for Salvatore's lofty frame to navigate, so, luckily, he would never venture there.

He expressed concern on discovering what I was up to, but I was defiant, and he accepted that he would find me there when I wasn't in the kitchen or out in the withered garden gathering up the last of the herbs I hung to dry in my attic or the seeds from rotting vegetables I saved to plant in spring. He found contentment in caring for the turkeys, grinding corn for feed, and in collecting the purple grapes, whose vines he pruned and trained in the rectangular arbor as big as a room. There was much to do on this carefully arranged farm that appeared frozen in time, as though someone had been living a most idyllic life there but had abruptly picked up and left. Or perhaps that person had intentionally made the property attractive to a caretaker to keep up appearances—or to distract from the real business at hand.

It was in the attic where I found my greatest treasure: the treadle sewing machine. On the wall, a board with dowels held thirty or forty spools of thread. What good fortune! Our luck was unending. With scraps of wool and cotton fabric I found lying on the rough plank floor, I made a quilt and clothing for the baby. From several bolts of cloth that had been enjoyed by moths, I sewed shirts for Salvatore and aprons and skirts for myself, embroidering birds or flowers or letters to hide the damage done by the insects. What I did was not extraordinary: all the young women in my village could do the same, all the while thinking it was peasants' work that lacked skill and intelligence. And we were foolish enough to believe such notions.

Since Salvatore had grown up on a pig and chicken farm, handling the turkeys came easily to him. He found boards and wire in the shed and built pens for rabbits and pigeons that he would raise for us to eat along with the turkeys, whose throats we slit and whose feathers we plucked because they were unsuitable in some way for the slaughterhouse. He created a path that led to an open hearth where, in warm weather, I would be able to roast our birds and pigs. On Thursdays he drove his horse and wagon into town and picked up what he needed from Mr. Martin—a tin of coffee beans, a cake of yeast, a large wedge of cheese—which Mr. Martin put on what he called a "tab" that the landlord took care of. Salvatore watched men in overalls and plaid work shirts take mail out of small boxes with secret combinations, content that no letters ever came for him. He tipped his hat and avoided eye contact with state police who stopped by Miller's store for a cup of freshly brewed coffee. They never paid, and Salvatore began to realize that things were not so different here than they were back in Calabria.

* * *

On a dreary January morning, I watched a skidding car suddenly emerge from the lower reaches of the hill. That's how it was, whether people walked or drove; they couldn't be seen until they had climbed the steep road that branched off from a wider one, dotted with other farms, that led to the main route. Unable to come any closer lest they got stuck, two figures trudged a good distance to the house through seven inches of newly fallen snow. One was broad, with a long fur coat and a felt hat that fit squarely on her head like a helmet, nearly covering her eyes. A smaller fur-clad figure trailed behind. Like a mamma bear and her cub, they barreled along the barely visible path.

Over coffee I poured from a white enamel pot and freshly baked *taralli* cookies and jam, Mrs. Carlson, a social worker, through Adela (who had not visited since the day of our arrival), tried to convince me to go to the Settlement House for Immigrants in the nearby city of Pohansac.

"We will teach you English, how to sew, cook, and manage money, care for your child, how to navigate the American system. Assimilate," Mrs. Carlson said, nodding to my big belly.

"Adapt," Adela said in Italian. "They'll try to convert you to Protestantism," she added, winking, to let me know they were her own words and not those of Mrs. Carlson.

I thanked Mrs. Carlson, explaining that I already knew how to do most of those things. After all, she was drinking my coffee and eating my cookies and the *marmellata* I had made from blackberries I'd picked. "But," I told Adela, "I *would* like to learn to speak and read and write English."

"Maybe it's best that you don't travel in this weather, in your condition. That you wait until spring, until after your baby is born," Mrs. Carlson said, conceding. "Perhaps Adela can work with you?" She looked Adela's way. "We can pay you, Adela."

Adela said that her husband had a car and came to Millers Falls once a week to distribute rotten lettuce thrown out by Pohansac grocers to the local farmers, who used it to feed their rabbits. He could drop her at the bottom of the road, do his business, and return for her when he was through.

"*Your* husband is a big man," Mrs. Carlson said to me, slipping into her bearskin coat and, from the kitchen window, watching Salvatore make his way across the open field with an armful of branches for kindling. "He treats you well? A lot of the men—they have heavy hands, especially when they drink. Does your husband drink?"

I caught Adela's wide-eyed warning as she translated, clearly fearing that even one revealing word I might have uttered in Italian might be detected by Mrs. Carlson. Adela knew perfectly well that Salvatore had to be making wine from the grapes in the arbor. Truth be told, he had found the hidden cellar beneath the heavy trap door in our bedroom, with a glass vat and large barrel inside: perfect for crushing grapes by hand and then storing their product. And, yes, we had learned that the sale and purchase of alcohol was outlawed in America, but we would never have bought or sold it. Still, Adela was making it clear that it behooved us to not to raise any suspicions regarding the contents of our cellar.

"No," I replied, lying about the drinking—though Salvatore never drank in excess—but not about Salvatore treating me well.

"Good." I could tell she liked the idea of Adela coming to the house and checking on the giant's wife.

"Is there a tub in the house?" Mrs. Carlson asked through Adela.

"Oh, yes!" I answered with pride.

"It would be good to use it before you come to the settlement house, whenever you do come." These were instructions. Adela hesitated to translate, then said, "How fortunate. You are a lucky couple."

And so every Friday morning, I pulled back the lacy curtain I had made from the scraps in the attic and watched tiny Adela, my first friend in America, trudge up the hill because her husband refused to drive her all the way—always with the excuse of getting stuck in snow or mud or whatever, Adela said.

* * *

Adela's husband did make it up the hill on a rainy Friday evening in April, with the midwife seated beside him. Having come earlier that afternoon for her weekly visit, it had not taken Adela long to assess the situation and announce that our baby would most assuredly be arriving before midnight. Instructing Salvatore to see to it that there was enough dry wood in the kitchen to feed the stove for boiling water, she gathered the necessities and plied me with tea brewed from the jar of dried mint on my windowsill. When her husband came to pick her up, she sent him to collect the midwife.

It was an easy birth, and I resolved to fill the house with babies for as long as my body allowed. We had crossed an ocean, survived snowstorms and sniffles, loneliness and confusion; we had reached the other side and had been rewarded. But it was not enough to remove the ever-present weight of guilt from Salvatore's shoulders.

"I saw you the other day," he told me several weeks later as I hung diapers on the line that stretched between two cherry trees, his voice filled more with disappointment than anger.

"You saw me where?"

"Heading down the other side of the hill toward the forbidden coops."

"It wasn't me, *caru miu*. I've never gone there. I don't care what they're doing, and I certainly don't want to be part of it. What was I wearing?" I asked, teasing.

"It was late, almost dark, and I couldn't tell because it was also a dark color. Maybe black."

"Well, if you couldn't see, you probably didn't see anything but the shadow of an animal. Perhaps a deer."

"Maybe you're right," he said, letting out a relieved laugh. He picked up the baby from the blanket she was lying on and walked toward the house. "Let's go in. The noise from the traffic is bound to wake the baby before those roosters do."

The noise to which he referred would come not from the clucking of chickens but from the engines of pickup trucks and their cargoes of rattling glass bottles as they left the coops before dawn several nights a month and made their way back up the hill. It hadn't taken us long to figure out what the men who drove the trucks were doing, but we minded our own business until the day my curiosity and brazenness got the better of me.

"What do you do there?" I asked the landlord's son, Paulie, when he handed me the fresh eggs he usually brought after a night down at the coops. He smiled, and for a moment I thought he would spill it all, but then he caught himself with a restraint most appealing to me, since I'd never known a man who didn't like to tell women things he thought they didn't know.

"You're very beautiful," he said instead. "*Bedda.* Isn't that the word?" he asked, clearly referring to the endearing term he'd heard me use for baby Lucia, who lay on a blanket near the stove, legs kicking off the woolen afghan Adela had crocheted for her, hands waving the dishrag I had given her to play with.

I nodded and offered him a cup of coffee and some *taralli*, keeping my back to him, no matter how offensive it might have seemed, because Paulie was much shorter than Salvatore and it would have been inevitable that our eyes would lock. But he was in a hurry.

"Next Thursday must be time for your husband to bring the turkeys to the slaughterhouse," he said.

He knew very well that was the day Salvatore would be gone, because Salvatore was always gone when he stopped by, and he always came on Thursdays. He also knew how to stir up a slow, burning desire for what I might never have wanted from him had he taken liberties too soon.

There was no need for Salvatore to tell me how much he wanted me: the semen I occasionally found on his pants revealed how he thought about me when he tilled the garden or fed the turkeys and got so excited that he turned to his own body to satisfy his yearnings. *I* had been the greatest temptation to his lust. *I* had pulled him away from his calling. *I* was what he tenderly referred to as his most blessed curse. Nevertheless, in bed, I like to ask, "Am I desirable to you?" And, devouring me, he would answer that childbearing had only enhanced me, matured me, ripened me to the point that I was softer and moister and more irresistible than the plumpest tomato. When you thrive on superlatives, nothing ever seems to be enough; they only feed your need for more.

* * *

I compared every aspect of Paulie to Salvatore: his sandy hair, blue eyes, narrow nose and chin. Unlike my husband's face, no particular feature demanded attention. He smelled as though he had just come from the barbershop; Salvatore bathed perhaps once a week and rarely changed his clothes since he had so few. One day, as Paulie handed me the basket, he gently caressed my cheek, and I smelled— not from his breath but his calloused hands—the sweet scent of gin. "*Bedda*," he murmured. "The *most* beautiful," he continued, as though entranced. I turned away as his fingers moved from my cheek to my temple, not to be coy this time, but to stop him from sweeping back the lock of hair I draped over my discoloration—the brown spots I had received as an infant when my older sister, sitting by the fireplace, accidentally dropped me into a pile of glowing ashes. My seeming rebuff only fed his determination; we were alike, Paulie and I. When Adela showed up unexpectedly during one of Paulie's visits, both guests appeared ready to wait the other out.

"Watch that one," Adela said after Paulie finally left.

"He is bad?" I asked, not sure what interpretation of the word I had in mind.

"No," she said. "That's the problem. He's one of the better ones."

The following week, the baby was napping soundly in the bedroom when Paulie delivered the eggs and a bottle of perfume. I had fed and rocked her and sung her to sleep. As I said, we were of like minds, Paulie and I. The perfume gave me the perfect excuse to throw my arms around his neck. He, in turn, wrapped his around my waist, and we kissed—lightly at first, then passionately, leaning into one another and pressing hard until we reached satisfaction. "No more," I said, faintly protesting. "Never again." Yet Paulie returned each week, daring to lift the folds of my long cotton dress and, sometimes in plain sight of the wide-eyed infant who watched with innocent curiosity, played with me as I pushed and twisted against him.

I told Salvatore that the perfume had come from Adela. I began to wash more often, particularly on the days Salvatore left the farm. And I made sure to make love to him on those nights—to assure him, and myself, just as I had in the sacristy in Fossato Serralta, that all was as it should be. And, truth be told, I was clever not to lie to Salvatore.

"I saw you!" Salvatore accused me with an anger of which I'd thought him incapable. He had come from the fields and stormed into the house the evening of the day I had led Paulie up the attic steps to the makeshift mattress fashioned from a pile of quilts.

"What do you mean?" I asked, my mind zigzagging in every direction that offered some nonsensical excuse for what he might have seen, but unable to temper the heat rising to my face.

"Going down the hill toward the forbidden coops. I saw you again! What are you trying to do? Get us evicted?"

"I haven't been to the coops, *ever!*" I said, blurting out the words, relieved. "In all this time I swear to you, Salvatore, I have never gone down to the coops. I don't care about the coops. I have Lucia and enough work to keep me occupied. I—"

"Another deer—perhaps," he said, distressed. "But it was earlier this time. I could swear it was you. In that same black dress."

"My love, I don't have a black dress. You see things no one else does. And you worry far too much."

With that, he shook his head in frustration at the inexplicable queerness of it all, finished his wine, and brought Lucia to his lap.

I couldn't stop thinking about Paulie day and night, and about how clever I was to be able to have not one but two men adore me: two men who more than met my growing needs, fueled by their own desires. During our short but exciting times in the attic, Paulie professed his love for me over and over. He would do anything, he said, anything if I would leave Salvatore—even though he knew his father would never approve of me, an immigrant of the lowest order. Had I interpreted his words and sincerity correctly, or had I fashioned them to my own liking? My desire for this man, who appeared grander and more knowledgeable simply because he belonged to this world in which we had landed, began to chip away at my love for Salvatore. This alienation deepened due to the pessimism that settled on Salvatore after Lucia's birth: suspicious apparitions, fear for Lucia's and my safety, a weight in the form of real pain that pressed down on his shoulders. And while I fantasized about a life with Paulie, it was the sense of the power I wielded in controlling two men that excited me most.

* * *

It was sleeting the night eight-month-old Lucia spiked a fever. I had done all I knew how to do throughout the day: bathed her in cold water, kept cool cloths on her forehead, put a mustard plaster on her chest to break up the congestion that made it difficult for her to breathe. "We need to take her to the pharmacist," I said to Salvatore. He assured me that we would never make it all the way to Pohansac in the single-digit temperatures that would surely cause us all to catch pneumonia—especially me, now five months pregnant, and Lucia. "*Aspett*," he said. Wait. Then he knelt beside the crib he had constructed and prayed.

Despite the weather, the trucks with giant chains on their tires began to venture up the hill and I took heart.

"The men down at the coops—they have vehicles. They can take us to the pharmacist. They can bring a doctor."

Still he would not go. When I put on my coat and headed for the door, he stopped me, went for his own jacket and galoshes, and headed down the other side of the hill. But he returned alone—wet, deflated, and humiliated. He had begged, and the landlord had refused. Paulie had offered to go, giving Salvatore hope, daring to tell the father that someone *should* go, but the father forbade him to leave until morning, after they had finished their work and made their deliveries, and the son had conceded.

The sleet turned to snow; the baby grew listless; the caravan made its way back from the coops. Elation turned to tears as the pickup trucks passed the house and continued down the other side of the hill toward town, leaving the echo of rattling bottles and chains. It was nine in the morning when Paulie returned with a doctor who took one look at Lucia and, without bothering to take out his stethoscope, confirmed what we knew.

"You came for me too late," he said, gesturing to her blue color and troubled breathing. The death rattle, he called it; the sound of diphtheria closing in.

The baby was buried in the small cemetery in town. Adela and the women from the settlement house arranged everything, from the white casket that had sat on our white-linen-draped kitchen table for the three-day wake to the spray of white flowers that hung on our front door, over which had passed the angel of death. White. To signify the innocence of the child who had been taken away. The women had also—probably at the urging of Adela—arranged not for a Protestant minister but for the Catholic priest from Pohansac, the cleric Salvatore had formerly dreaded confronting but who now gave not the slightest inkling of recognizing Salvatore as one of his own. I have little remembrance of the few who came to pay their respects, except that Paulie was not among them.

I locked the door when Paulie resumed bringing the eggs, which he now left on the steps. The next time the pickup trucks rumbled by, I cursed the men who drove them, threatening to go down to the coops and tear their eyes out.

"*Aspett*," Salvatore uttered yet again. Only this time he was devoid of fear, hollowed out by emotion.

It was around midnight when a different caravan tore up the northern side of the hill, headlights blazing, sirens wailing: a black Ford Model T from the sheriff's department, two from the state police, and several paddy wagons.

"Was it *you*?" I asked Salvatore, unable to believe he had brought on the raid.

"What does it matter? *È giustu.*" It was only right. He stated this coldly, staring at the empty cradle.

* * *

Salvatore and I floated in a haze during the winter and spring following Lucia's death. At night, we clung to one another in the safety of our bed, seeking comfort and consolation for ourselves more than for each other. Forgiveness was nowhere to be found: we were all among the guilty, the unfaithful. Salvatore viewed our loss as the inescapable punishment he had anticipated—his sin against God— that had only been compounded by his having also caused *me* to suffer. Paulie had been spared jail because he hadn't been at the coops on the night of the raid, yet I derived satisfaction in knowing that he was, according to Adela, one of the good ones. I hoped his inability to cross his father would forever haunt him as he continued to tend to the chickens and leave me eggs—to what end? To seek forgiveness? To lie with me again in the sanctuary of my attic?

Salvatore was in the stable with the horse on the evening I heard Paulie's car on its way to the coops. I stomped down the hill for the very first time, the ample folds of the black mourning dress Adela had given me, and that I had worn every day, in one hand, a kerosene lantern in the other. I rushed—my boots hitting the damp grass with a strange assuredness, as though they had passed that way a hundred times before. I rushed to get there before Salvatore became aware of my absence, before the arrival of the unborn child I carried, before I changed my mind.

Through the window of the old barn I could see him, still handsome, but the slender physique looking weak to me now as he moved about, opening and closing cages, as though unsure of what he was supposed to accomplish. When he looked up and saw me his eyes widened in surprise. He smiled. That's when I threw the lantern through one of the broken windows and onto the hay-covered floor of the structure now empty of the stills that had been seized, the mighty secret it had harbored. A structure containing nothing more than a few chickens and a regretful man seeking solace or repentance—which, I would never know. A man who, though capable of fleeing in time to save himself, would never reach me as I climbed back up the hill, my way now lit by the glow of flames, well aware of what I already knew: no matter the magnitude of the conflagration, our misdeeds would never be erased.

I dream about my lover from time to time, but he appears in no greater detail than those sketches of men with untraceable pasts, men whose stories I cannot flesh out, whose lives I can no longer mesh with mine. He has become unrecognizable to me. Like me—like Salvatore—he is different. Changed. He is a man who walks in dreams only.

The Woman Who Drew on Walls

My mother was an artist, although she didn't know it. "I just like to draw," she would say, implying that there was no correlation between her enjoyment and her talent. In fact, she didn't believe she possessed any talent at all. "I doodle," she said. But no one I knew doodled with the intricacy that my mother did. My friends' mothers left pads filled with stars or three-dimensional squares or fancy script, at best, on their telephone tables. My mother left pages of complex and incomprehensible figures—animate and inanimate, earthly and alien, familiar objects and those yet to be invented—that evoked peace, or howled confusion and rage.

I remember one picture that she painted on the wall in the small foyer of our apartment that frightened me. Taller than I was at the age of four, and several feet wide, it depicted a two-headed individual in a T-shirt and jeans, its gender indecipherable. Half of the person was serene and comely, but the other frantically screamed, disheveled hair ablaze, its arms flailing about, stirring something within me. That picture cost us our security deposit when we had to relocate to a cheaper apartment, the landlord claiming that he not only would have to paint over the artwork but would have visit his doctor on several occasions to quell the disturbing thoughts the painting provoked.

My mother also liked to sing, especially at the deep basin of the double kitchen sink, where she scrubbed laundry against the rippled glass surface of a washboard and then hung the sheets, heavy with the weight of water, on the clothesline outside our kitchen window.

I would wrap my arms around her legs to anchor her, fearing the sheets would pull her down three stories into the narrow concrete alley, and that I would lose her as I had the father who'd sailed to his death from the girder of a Manhattan construction site when I was ten, forever changing our lives. I remember my mother alongside him on the piano bench in our tiny Brooklyn apartment, in a room crowded with her sisters and with cousins with ample breasts forcing their way out of low-cut polished cotton sheaths, their dark hair cut in the trendy style of an artichoke and their husbands with bellies too distended for their age. Several of their offspring lay head to toe with me on my full-sized bed, listening to the adults singing and laughing behind the closed door of the adjacent room while we pretended to be asleep.

The music of Sinatra and Bennett, and the laughter, might have been what kept the others awake, but for me it was the anticipation of what the morning would bring because the evening was sure to prompt a deep sleep for my exhausted mother. She had hosted the event after a long week of taking dictation from a cantankerous boss and putting in overtime as a cleaning woman in that same office complex. Her deep sleep fostered good dreams, and good dreams resulted in pictures that would appear the following day, and for several days to come, in the most unpredictable places.

Looking for them was most of the fun, because she hid them to instill in me a sense of curiosity. Her images might appear on one side of the large box of Christmas ornaments hidden away behind the dust ruffle of my bed or, after my father passed, under the living room convertible sofa that doubled as my mother's bed; on the chalkboard easel she had given me for my birthday; on the white subway-style tile of the bathroom wall. We never failed to be penalized when we moved to smaller apartments, since she always drew in indelible ink or painted with acrylic or oil. Her siblings called her foolish and deemed the impetus for such behavior incomprehensible. Sometimes she labored on rolls of toilet paper that, when unraveled quickly like the frames of a movie tape, told a story of sorts. I say "of sorts" because her intent was never quite clear and was a source of both wonder and frustration to me. It would take me a long time—decades—to understand that the drawings were not renderings of the past or present but rather of the future, of situations not created by her imagination but predetermined and unknown to her at the time.

* * *

Nowadays, she often calls me in the late hours wanting to know where her daughter is. Her daughter is long gone; it's me, her son, that she's speaking to. But it's my father she's missing tonight. Have I heard from him? He must be with another woman! "He doesn't sleep with the woman," my mother says to assure me. "But then where *does* he sleep?" she asks. "He should be here in *my* bed." She's angry that he hasn't come home. But she's also worried. And why aren't *I* home by now? She says she can't stay up all night worrying about me, too. When I go to her, she is still frantic though exhausted, eyes bloodshot and tearing. "Go upstairs!" she says, trembling fingers combing matted gray hair. "Don't sleep anywhere else but home." I offer her a dose of Ativan with some water. After several refusals, she begrudgingly concedes and collapses onto her bed. There is no "upstairs" for me to go to; she lives in one room on the first floor of the assisted living complex. I climb into the bed and lie next to her, patting her sweaty brow, smoothing her covers until she falls asleep.

* * *

I miss the drawings. She hasn't made one in almost twenty years. They were once a godsend to us: a prosperous client of the accounting firm where she was employed found one in the men's room that she had cleaned the night before. "Who did this?" he asked my mother's boss. The only other person who had been in the bathroom had been Iris, the boss said, but she only cleaned it. "Anyone who can draw like this must come to work for me," the client said, insistent, leaving her boss confused and taken aback. My mother was a good worker, and class-A stenographer, typist, and book-keeper. Her boss underpaid her and didn't want to lose her. My mother, fearful of causing an uproar, denied having done the art-work, but the client didn't believe her. He insisted that she draw something on a blank piece of company letterhead right there and then.

"I can't," she said. "I only fiddle around."

"Please try."

"What should I draw?"

"Anything. A house—a very fancy house in the country. A flock of birds in a meadow."

Nervous, she drew some rudimentary strokes, a scene that could have been created by any elementary schoolchild—by me.

The client was confused. The boss said he had told him so.

"Then where did the drawings come from?" the client asked.

"I have no idea, but we'll have to paint over them before the property manager sees them." The boss didn't mask his annoyance.

When the client returned several weeks later to retrieve his pre-pared tax return, he made sure to go to the men's room, where he found more artwork in another stall. This one was in pastel chalk—*my* chalk, with which I created hopscotch courts on the sidewalk or crushed in a handkerchief and threw against apartment building stoops the night before Halloween, leaving starbursts of color.

"Ask her to open her desk drawers," the client said, instructing my mother's boss, who complied because this man was a valued customer.

When the client saw the pink and blue and yellow pieces of chalk, he asked her why she denied having made the drawings.

"Because—I don't know. I don't know where they come from. I get the urge, and the next moment I'm doing them. But I can't duplicate them. I don't even know what they mean."

"They're beautiful," he said. "Outstanding. Reminiscent of Chagall, but more abstract and intricate like Picasso. Organic like Morris with a contemporary, hallucinogenic twist. You must be on drugs," he said—an assumption she vehemently denied. "I love that they are so open to interpretation. They give me a sense of right being left, of up being down, of things turned inside out, of layers upon layers. They make me wonder—struggle to decipher meaning: Where does the path lead? Is it a path at all? Are these animate figures or figments of my imagination? This is the stuff people can look at forever. This is what people crave. This is what one must do with wallpaper: stare at it endlessly with renewed pleasure. You must come to work for me."

"Doing what?" she asked.

"Creating artwork that designer wallpaper companies want."

"I don't know the first thing about creating wallpaper."

"That's not your job. What you need to know, I'll teach you, with the proviso that you paint on our walls when prompted."

* * *

I get a call around 5 p.m. "Your mother won't go to the dining room for supper," Maria, the certified nursing assistant, or CNA as they're called, says. "She's waiting for her husband Bill. Says she never eats without him." When I get to her apartment, I find notes in various locations: on the small table where she likes to sit; on the cabinet door above the stove that's been turned off ever since she charred a pot on the electric burner, setting off terrifying alarms and filling the halls with smoke. "You'll have to pay for the damage," they say. "Of course," I say, to assure them, knowing that this is a dreaded precursor to their urging me to move her to the memory unit.

I bring her a box of cream-and-nut-filled chocolates, the kind my father would give her on Valentine's Day but inside a brilliant red heart. She says I'm her shining star. Then she reverts to my father's sleeping around with other women, to his never having slept one night in her bed since he took her to this new place on the night they were married, to his never having given her a cent.

"Thank goodness they don't ask for money here," she says. "I've got to think of where I'm going to go. I can't drive to shop for milk and other groceries. I shouldn't have sold my car. I have to get a job."

I ask if I should remove the large photo she has of my dad as a serviceman, but she says no, even though she insists that no one would believe what he became—they always thought he was so kind and good.

"Do you see him?" I ask her.

"Sometimes. But he never says anything. Sometimes I miss him."

"But do you *see* him?"

"Yes, sometimes. But he just comes and goes." She dismisses his behavior with the wave of a hand. There are days when she sort of knows me as I am—her only child, her son.

"Where's your sister?" she asks.

"She's gone away," I say.

"She was nice. I liked her. But you're nice too." She smiles, then says, "I'm worried about Mama." Now I'm her sibling.

"She's fine," I say. Dead and buried over thirty years ago.

"Papa beats her, you know."

"Oh, I don't think so."

"Yes. I know so."

She often disparages the men in her life who were, for the most part, good men. And while grandfather may have had an explosive disposition, it's the one time he slapped my grandmother and was warned that she would leave him if he ever did it again that has turned him into a monster in my mother's mind.

I tell her to instruct my father to never come back, hoping that will mitigate her anxiety and hallucinations, yet I fear I'm betraying the father I knew only to be good. He understands, I tell myself, that I must do it for her sake, but if I think too much about it— about the happy way they were—I cry.

"Okay," she says, agreeing for now. "Someday I'll run into your father, and I'll just say, 'Oh, hi, Bill'," she says, coolly. The only thing that would make it cooler was if she were smoking a cigarette.

She regularly brings back leftovers from the dining room—a piece of nibbled-at cake, half a sandwich, two pats of butter, melted ice cream—for her mother to eat when she returns home from work.

One evening I find her alone, hugging a teddy bear in a red velvet jacket with brass buttons as she sits in the dark in the empty activities room, waiting for a movie to be shown. According to the daily notices in the hall, there is no movie tonight. She whimpers as though in physical distress.

"Does something hurt?" I ask.

She nods.

"Your foot or your leg?"

"My right."

"Yes, but of what?"

"My left."

"Your left leg?"

"My back. I'll never be able to have children. I know it. I'll have to adopt."

"Do you know how old you are?"

"No."

"Eighty-six."

"I am?"

"Yes."

"Will you take him with you?" She holds out the teddy bear. She has always had a penchant for stuffed animals, and the teddy is her favorite. "Really, he needs to see the world. He's no bother."

Her smile leads me to believe that she knows he isn't real, that she is toying with me. Still, the persistence of her playful behavior makes me understand that, like a child, she isn't quite sure.

"He would miss you," I say. "He needs to be with you."

Later that night I listen to a voicemail from her on my phone.

"What's happening?" she asks, crying. "Will someone tell me what's happening!"

What *is* happening? I ask myself.

* * *

"She won't come to dinner again," says a staff member who phones me the next day. "She's pacing the halls, waiting for Bill."

When I try to convince her to go and eat, she says he's at it again, gambling and drinking. Out with that other woman.

"Then just forget him," I say. "Take care of yourself. You owe it to yourself after all these years. Have supper."

"I can't go without him." She is adamant.

The following morning I arrive to take her to a doctor's appointment, but she tells me that she can't go because someone just called to say they were taking her somewhere.

"Mom," I say. "It was me. *I* called."

* * *

When she first went to work for the client's art studio, my mother was gripped by artist's block.

Her new boss wasn't concerned. "How about you bring me whatever you draw or paint at home. On whatever you do it on. We can reproduce it."

She brought in what was portable: boxes and scraps of paper, the blank pages of bound books, the rewound rolls of toilet paper—all with their depictions of small floating objects that resembled walkie-talkies but that were much smaller, wizards flying on broomsticks through thick forests, miniature aerodynamic cars, leopards tucked away among palm fronds and colorful birds of paradise, tigers with metallic gold stripes swimming in blue waves along with silvery-centered octopuses, and dense, giant roses unlike any I'd ever seen in our neighborhood. She copied them onto thirty-by-thirty-six-inch sheets of paper with layer upon layer of acrylic paint, each adding greater dimension to the painting, greater detail, and more color. Graphic design directors were wild about the shimmering gold forests and geometric figures on matte backgrounds when they came searching for something innovative for their wall coverings. Her glittering foil patterns and embossed cabbage roses became all the rage in the seventies and were copied by everyone. Before long, her designs showed up on bedding and ceramic tiles.

Occasionally she left new drawings in the restroom, and her boss encouraged her to embellish them right there before she rendered them on the large sheets. And when she couldn't come up with something fresh and unconventional, she drew inspiration from the conventional artwork of those who had come before her, adding some novel twist to avoid copyright issues, something quirky that always enhanced the original and never detracted from the finished product.

Everyone assumed she preferred her new job to the old one, but when asked what they thought was a rhetorical question, she simply shrugged. "I liked my old job too. I liked the secret world of shorthand no one else could decipher. I liked my fingers flying on the typewriter faster than anyone else's. I liked the satisfaction of turning a dirty toilet into a sparkling one." She was gifted with the ability to find satisfaction in anything she labored at. But this job left her with more money and time for her daughter (that is, me, her son). She liked that above all else. When she retired, she said she had been turned off by the appearance of the first digital collection of giant-sized flowers and other grotesque fauna, but I think she was a bit intimidated by the new technology she feared would overtake the old art form—and she was tired.

* * *

"How long have you known?" she asked when I told her of my decision to transition. "Before the *schizophrenic* painting"—which we had come to call the two-headed figure—"or after?"

"Let's say I always knew something was up from the get-go. Like never being able to find anything in my wardrobe I felt comfortable in. Only it was more than that. It was skin. But I must admit, even after the painting appeared, I still wasn't convinced. I tried *not* to be convinced. All that daddy's-little-girl stuff and everything."

"Did the painting *help* to convince you?"

"Not right away. But, I guess, in the end, yes."

"Good." She smiles. "I'm glad it was a help."

"Did you know then? When you did the painting?" I asked.

"I should have, but, no, I didn't. I'm sorry."

"Then—"

"I don't know where it came from. I can say my subconscious, but I'd probably be lying."

She was on board as far as helping me was concerned. She researched, and she consulted every professional she could. She told me I was brave. It took years for me to begin to comprehend the strength and compassion it must have taken her to be brave.

"Too bad about the name," she said.

"Well, I couldn't go around as Camille."

"Your father's choice. To be honest, I don't miss it." This kind of offends me. "I like Charlie better," she says.

* * *

Sometimes, when she remembers I'm her offspring and not her sister—but not necessarily her son—she tells me she had me out of wedlock. She doesn't remember how it happened, since she insists that she never had sex before marriage. And, to their credit, her parents and other relatives didn't treat her badly because of it. But she can't recall ever getting married despite the wedding photo on her dresser, only buying the dress.

"I married a nice man," she says as follow-up, adding to my confusion. "Your father. Well, he's not your father."

It's those instances that leave me doubting things I've accepted as truth, although I know there's no need to question any of it. I know this when I find her brushing toothpaste on her eyebrows or washing her soiled disposable diapers and hanging them to dry on the walker she's mistaken for a towel rack, all the while telling me she's getting ready for her new job as a caregiver for an elderly woman. She wants to know what she should charge. I know there's no need to doubt her when she asks me who her husband was, and when I tell her it was Bill, she says, "You know I wasn't married!" Or when, for the second time in a day, I find every article of clothing displayed on her bed—drawers and closet empty. "Time for us to move again," she says. Or when I apply expensive compression bandaging she's pulled down her swollen legs and ruined three hours after I put on the first pair, and she tells me I'm stupid. That those of us around her are all so very stupid.

I know there's no need to confirm anything when they tell me that they found her sitting on a bench in the courtyard at 3 a.m. and eating an apple after she'd found a way to open the sliding door that staff members must climb onto a footstool to unlock.

* * *

I'm sound asleep on the winter evening I get the call.

"There's been an accident. Your mother needs to go to the hospital. She's bleeding. There's blood everywhere." The young woman speaking is a newly hired CNA. She is nervous. This is her first night shift alone, and she is struggling to remain composed. "I called an ambulance."

"Where should I meet her?" I ask.

"The hospital would be best. The ambulance will be here any minute."

I should have gone to her residence because I wait at the ER entrance for thirty minutes before the gurney is wheeled in. I go through the necessary admission procedure, responding to questions whose answers already exist in their records because I've answered them countless times before; my mother insisting that I am the patient, not her, that she is only accompanying me.

There is a dark, gaping hole in her forehead and scratches caked with blood on her face. A technician hooks her up to monitoring machines; EKG electrodes are taped onto various parts of her body. She takes her temperature, blood pressure, and other vitals. How did it happen? she asks. How did it happen? the nurse who comes in after a long while asks. How did it happen? the doctor who comes in after an even longer time and, ignoring the nurse's notes, asks.

"She fell onto a bedside table that collapsed. The lamp on it was glass. That's all I know," I tell each one of them.

"So, she was stabbed," the doctor says to confirm.

"I guess so," I say.

"Why are you asking her all these questions?" my mother says. "Why don't you ask me?"

"Can you tell me what happened?"

"I really don't remember, except that I got myself off the floor and walked for help."

"That's true," I say. "They said she wandered in her bloodstained nightgown all the way to the nurses' station on the other side of the building." The thought deeply upsets me.

"You must have passed out," the doctor says.

She nods.

He requests X-rays of her brain. The orderly doesn't arrive to take her to imaging for another ninety minutes.

"Why don't you eat something?" my mother says.

"The cafeteria is closed."

"There must be food somewhere. A machine maybe."

"I had dinner."

"But that was hours ago. You must be hungry now. What did you eat?"

"Tofu and scrambled eggs."

"I don't like what you ate."

"You didn't eat it."

She laughs. "I know it's healthy. I always tried to feed you healthy foods. I haven't kept up with the latest trends the way I used to."

"You did fine, Mom," I say sincerely, remembering the yogurt, blackstrap molasses, and wheat germ she kept in the refrigerator after having voraciously read Adelle Davis's *Let's Eat Right to Keep Fit* and Gayelord Hauser's *Look Younger, Live Longer*.

"I miss him—your father. He was so good. So good."

"He was," I say, a bit stunned at the compliment she's paid him but grateful for her awareness. "We were lucky to have him."

"Yes." She smiles and reaches for my hand.

The nurse returns to suture the deep wound. My mother is brave, barely flinches.

"Can we go home now?" she asks when she finishes.

"We have to wait until we get the X-ray results."

"Drab," she says, eyeing the cream-colored walls and gray floors.

"The room next door is peach."

"Boring. Look at the scuff marks. This trend away from wallpaper is a mistake. When I wake up, I hope it's over."

With that she falls into a deep sleep. I try to doze but the only chair in the room is utterly uncomfortable without a headrest. I could climb into the hospital bed with her, but I don't want to disturb her. I try various ways of supporting my head, but none work. I can't sleep.

At 4:30 a.m., the nurse pops in again with the results: no skull fractures, no concussion.

"Can we go home?" my mother asks again.

"As soon as we complete the discharge papers."

My mother falls asleep for another hour, then wakes with a searing statement.

"Charlie, I just realized I have no clothes!"

"Oh Mom, you're right! They didn't send you here with a coat or shoes! Just your nightie! It's freezing outside."

"Guess they didn't think I'd be returning." She laughs.

"You can have my jacket."

"You know it wouldn't cover a quarter of me, you're so skinny!"

"We'll have to wrap you up in some hospital blankets. At least they're big—and warm. I'll pull up to the entrance of your place and you won't have to walk too far in the snow in those hideous, orange nonskid socks!"

"Thank God it's still dark outside!" she says. "No one will see me. Those blankets are so white and worn. Like giant diapers. You know I like to be stylish."

And with that we burst into laughter as I ring for the technician who hooked her up to the monitors, cleaned her soiled sheets, mopped her accident, and did almost every unpleasant task, including taking her to the bathroom one last time. I assure the nurse that I'll return the blankets, and before daybreak my mother is miraculously back in her own apartment. I get chills seeing the remains of the accident that has yet to be cleaned up: the large, bloodstained shard of the glass lamp that punctured her upper forehead and sank an inch deep; the fragments of glass that her face lay on for who knows how long until she regained consciousness.

And it hits me that, despite this horrific experience, or perhaps because of it, she and I have been having normal exchanges throughout the night. Iris has been lucid, making a jolly time of the event, much the way she used to when adversity came knocking. And I think a miracle of sorts has happened: the incision of the glass, the blow to the head, has somehow righted her condition. Wasn't that how Lasik eye surgery was discovered? A Russian worker's cornea accidentally cut up from bits of shattered glass resulted in correcting his nearsightedness? Why not with dementia? The nerves to the brain repaired; its patchy spots and frontal lobe regenerated; its eventual regrowth.

I'm flying high as I get ready for work. I sing in the shower. I plan my next vacation. I'm free. I'm putting on my favorite outfit when the hospital calls.

"We have a most unusual circumstance."

"You need the blankets."

"Your mother has defiled the bathroom. She drew on the walls with black markers that were hanging from the staff's whiteboard in there."

"Why do you have a whiteboard in the bathroom?"

"That's not your concern."

She had spent a long time in there. "I'm sure it's a big improvement over your nondescript décor."

"That too is none of your concern."

"Look, she has dementia. What can I tell you?"

"Well, it does have the looniness of someone not in complete possession of their faculties all right. Though I must admit it's quite lovely in its own way. Lovely and terrifying."

I let out a sigh of exasperation. "Okay. Enough. I do not believe it's my responsibility. Check with housekeeping. Or the hospital's insurance company." I will never set foot in the place again.

A few hours later I receive a text from a hospital administrator telling me I can hire a painter or paint the walls myself. Absurd. She has attached a photo of the crime scene, which I blow up to see more clearly. A child. A boy. Much like the schizophrenic one of old. Only this one has a single head. A male with short, spiked hair much like my own, except that his head is disproportionately small for his body. And while the boy flails his arms in some terror, his eyes look upward. His world is spinning around him—the entire background is smeared as though in motion, whizzing by: unrecognizable, incomprehensible. He is lost. And this, I know, is my future. A world of detachment. Of solitude. Of confusion.

When the familiar tune of my phone sounds that evening, I hesitate to answer. I can't be with her now that she is whole, knowing what I know. Perhaps it will even be early onset for me: the tables turned, and once again *she* will be the caregiver. We are tied together—always have been. Mother and son. Son and mother.

"Iris won't go to dinner," yet another new staffer says. "She's roaming the halls, knocking on doors, bothering everyone, asking for him."

"For who?" I ask, not wanting to know.

"The man she's waiting for. Bill. The man she calls her husband."

For the Love of Buffaloes

Karl Siracconi stepped out of his snow-coated loafers and left them in the center of the mudroom for Marguerite to trip over. He wore his buttoned-up overcoat into the kitchen, where he stood immobile, staring ahead—at nothing. Not that there wasn't anything to see. Marguerite, his wife, was an interior designer, and their renovated Craftsman home could have rivaled any remake on the *Home Network* channel. But like his shoes that sat abandoned in the center of the slate-tiled mudroom despite Marguerite's having provided a designated cubby for them, Karl felt displaced. Miss Penelope, a ten-year-old calico Persian, appeared out of nowhere and, meowing for attention, brushed against his leg. He ignored her.

When he began to perspire, he took off his wet wool coat, draped it over the back of a hardwood stool, and sat at the island. Hands clasped as in prayer on the white marble counter, he continued to stare until the light coming in through the French doors that led to the patio turned an eerie blue and he heard his wife's attempt to unlock the already unlocked mudroom door.

He hadn't left work early due to the unpredicted snowfall: Western Mass Wealth Management only closed shop when forewarned of a natural disaster. He'd been at the firm for twenty-five years; seen the number of its employees swell; welcomed into the world forty-two of their children; and witnessed the death of its founder, Marcus Corcoran, who'd choked on a turkey club sandwich during a staff meeting. There'd been a lengthy summary of his accomplishments in the obituaries section of the locally syndicated newspaper, but that was all: no front-page article entitled *Founder of Successful Firm Chokes on Turkey Club*. Well, that would have been gauche, Karl had to admit. But this man who had managed to safeguard hundreds of retirement funds throughout several major financial crises, including the Great Recession of 2007, deserved more recognition.

Karl hated himself when he entertained thoughts like this. People were people. What was the need for fame? Did it bring happiness? It wasn't esteem Karl was searching for but a certain kind of satisfaction that propelled him out of bed each morning. One that quelled the restlessness in his weary limbs and left him spent at night.

"Where's your car?" Marguerite called from the mudroom. She unwound her purple mohair scarf and untied the sash of her black wrap coat. Next she unzipped the tall boots that defined her shapely legs so well they could have been custom made and not snatched off the sale rack at Macy's. He heard her kick his loafers into the boot pan under the bench. "Jeez, Karl," she muttered.

"I walked," he replied, his back to her.

"From where? Did you break down? Why didn't you call me?"

"Didn't break down," he said matter-of-factly. "At least my car didn't."

"How far did you walk?"

"From work."

"You walked four miles in this weather? What the hell's wrong with you?"

She came around the island and faced him. There was nothing fragile about this tall Nordic woman who was not afraid to get her hands dirty: stripping and painting furniture, hanging wallpaper, scrubbing toilets, composting garbage. He directed his dark brown eyes up toward her blue ones without moving a neck muscle. She was always good at cutting to the chase. Something was *very* wrong with him.

"It wasn't the walk. I enjoyed it," he said.

"You never walk to work when it's nice out, let alone twenty degrees. What's with you, Karl?" She leaned into the counter to get closer to him, and he could swear that her blond hair was actually a halo around her pale face, rosy from the cold.

"Are you sick?" She went around to him and felt his forehead with her hand. She should have used her lips, he thought; that's what his mother had always done. But Marguerite had never been a mother.

"I quit," he told the pretty angel of mercy.

"What?"

"I haven't said anything to anyone yet, but I'm not going back. I didn't go back after lunch. I'm not going back tomorrow. Or ever."

She nodded. "Okaaay, we'll talk about it."

"You don't understand, Marguerite. I'm empty."

"I see." And though she was never one to jump to conclusions, her eyes revealed that she understood only too well that things were about to change.

"It's not you—at least not only. It's … everything."

She nodded again. "I'll make dinner. We'll talk."

* * *

They ate pork chops Marguerite defrosted in the microwave, smothered with barbecue sauce and broiled, along with a side of mashed potatoes. She wasn't a gourmet cook but had mastered a repertoire of decent meals she could rustle up in no time. He had sat and watched her peel the potatoes with a determination that assured him she could do this—whatever it took, she would see them through it. She always turned to mashed potatoes when one of them needed comfort. Maybe she just liked venting her frustration as she came down hard on the little boiled chunks, smashing the crap out of them with a handheld masher. Maybe it was the warmed half-and-half or the butter she beat into them that promised a kind of reassurance like that of mother's milk. Whatever it was, these spuds were her go-to in times like this.

Marguerite waited out Karl as they ate in silence. Blessed with infinite patience, she could have been a disaster management specialist. Instead, she wasted her tranquil demeanor and grace on the petulant clientele whose homes she decorated.

Finally, he spoke. "Time is running out for me," he said, picking up the vintage crystal saltshaker and examining it—turning it round and round in one hand.

She nodded. "Time is always running out on us."

"But for me—it's really running out."

"Why do you say that?"

"Genes. My father died of cancer at fifty-three, just like *his* father."

"Your mother lived to seventy-two."

"Young in today's world."

"You're only forty-nine. That gives you at least four years, Mr. Downer. Even if you take after the males."

"That's encouraging," he said. But her comment was exactly what he had expected her to say, why he loved her—and at times resented her.

"So—what are you going to do about all this?" she asked as though he had just discovered a leak in the roof. She poured them both another glass of red wine.

"Give notice. Tomorrow."

"Is that fair? Pulling out on them like that?"

"I can handle a few clients from home until they turn them over to someone else. Today, tomorrow—it doesn't matter to them."

"Who's *them*?"

"Everyone."

"Okay then. That's a start."

"Yeah," he said, relaxing his shoulders for the first time that evening.

"I have to go to Boston tomorrow to look at a pair of Louis XV chairs for a couple in Lenox."

"Can't they send you a photo?"

"I need to examine them, sit in them. You know they lie about the condition. What do you say?"

"About what?"

"Can I leave you, Karl? Will you be all right alone?"

He shrugged.

"Jesus, Karl! Can you give me a straight answer?" He was exhausting even *her* patience.

"Sure," he said.

"You'll feel better after a good night's sleep. Why don't you take a bath?"

"I never take baths. Why would I take one now? Women take baths. Sick people take baths."

"It's relaxing."

"It's a waste of water."

"Fine. Take a shower—a long shower. Then go to bed."

"Don't worry about me, Margi."

"No," she said, gathering up the dishes and taking a deep breath. "I won't worry one bit. The snow seems to have let up. How about we pick up your car?" He nodded and rose to put on his jacket.

That night, husband and wife lay side by side, both knowing the other was awake yet pretending to sleep, both aware they had stumbled into one of those times when their marriage had assumed a life of its own and was just there, lying heavily between them.

* * *

In the morning he feigned sleep until she set out for Boston and then reached for his cell phone on the night table.

"Well, this comes as quite a surprise," Gunther Greene, the senior partner and current CEO, told him. He was prone to bullshitting. "You'll come in and say a proper goodbye to everyone, won't you, Karl?" It was a rhetorical question: Karl sensed enthusiasm in his superior's voice at the prospect of replacing a taciturn employee with a younger, more talented and gregarious coworker.

"We both know that's not necessary," Karl said as he rolled out of bed and headed to the bathroom. He might compose a handwritten note to the leader of first impressions (formerly known as the receptionist), maybe even invite her to lunch. He had admired her professionalism in the face of harassment from clients and several colleagues, and she had appreciated Karl's respect and support. There was no one else with whom he cared to break bread: in general, he didn't like people. "I'll certainly handle my clients until you're comfortable with a changeover."

"Not a problem," Gunther said. Karl knew that by the end of the day all of his clients would have been assigned to a new advisor. "Karl has moved on," they'd be told.

He didn't shower and, except for putting on a pair of boxers, didn't dress until noon, when he slipped into his oldest, most faded baggy jeans and a sweatshirt stained with paint and frayed at the seams. He didn't mind putting on a suit and tie for special occasions, but every day for twenty-five years had been cruel and unjust punishment. Best of all, he didn't shave, because shaving irritated the hell out of the fair skin he had inherited from his German mother. He didn't even comb his hair. He took every tube and jar of gel, wax, and paste he'd used to try to tame his black mop flecked with gray and tossed them into the wastebasket. "Goodbye, Don Draper, hello, Harry Potter," he told the image in the mirror.

He had time to make himself two eggs over easy on buttered rye toast instead of his usual bowl of Cheerios. Hell, he had time to bake himself a quiche! He poured a tall glass of orange juice and, while listening to a radio interview of a local writer, read the newspaper from the page one headlines to the sports section. Next he fetched the pen and Post-it pad Marguerite kept beside the landline: he'd have to come up with some way to earn a living, since they couldn't manage on Marguerite's earnings alone. Nothing came to mind.

"Take your time," Marguerite said when she phoned to see how he was doing, her voice breezy and sing-song. "Take a break. Do whatever makes you happy, brings you pleasure. You'll figure it out."

Either she was going to make a killing on those Louis XV chairs or she'd consulted a shrink. Or, better yet, a psychic.

He could go back to school, or take an online course, or apprentice in some field completely new to him. He was afraid of remaining idle for too long, afraid of sinking into depression. Although he'd never been clinically diagnosed, he sometimes got high—even manic—on a notion or activity that engaged him and then crashed when his expectations weren't fully met. Worse, he tended to direct that disappointment at Marguerite and on aspects of their marriage that had nothing to do with what had triggered his mood swing, just the little dissatisfactions with their lives, which he blew all out of proportion. He would update his LinkedIn profile: *Looking for a new venture—any venture.* Maybe hire a headhunter with a talent for soothsaying. Or he could hold off on employment and do whatever until he found something that really inspired him.

He put on his hiking boots and, with no destination in mind, started walking, moseying through streets lined with colorful clapboard homes, many of which dated back to the eighteenth or nineteenth century and whose interiors, Marguerite liked to remind him, had been updated six, seven, even eight times or more. Gables blanketed with snow and greenery in hibernation: they all looked the same to him during winter. To his delight, he found himself facing two boulders that marked the entrance to one of the narrow woodland trails that took hikers to Gilbert Lake.

Crunching through the first snow of the season, up hills and down, he followed the trail markers, stepping off the path only once to make way for a lone cross-country skier who, like himself, wasn't at work. He basked in the stillness, aware that the only sounds he heard were his own. When he arrived at the lake, he swept the snow off a wooden bench and sat, grateful to the Trustees of Reservations, which owned and maintained this and other retreats like it. He was glad that he and Marguerite were members. He took in the vast frozen lake before him and photographed it with his cell, then wiped his runny nose on his sleeve. The air was cold and moist, signaling a new snowfall on the way, and it wasn't even December yet. He decided he'd hike more often, each time attempting a new trail: Mount Greylock, the Holyoke Range, even Mount Monadnock in New Hampshire. He imagined himself walking the entire Appalachian Trail, his lungs working hard until he felt his heart beating so fast it seemed about to burst from his chest, and his body tingling with energy when he came to a standstill, as it did now.

When he got home, he wanted to write about what he had experienced but was too excited and impatient for a lengthy description. He jotted down *hiking* on the pad of yellow Post-its. On the next sheet he wrote *trees* and on a third, *nature*. He tore off the little squares of paper and took them into the dining room, where he stuck them on the only wall that wasn't devoted to pictures.

Famished, Karl fixed himself a grilled cheese sandwich and an espresso, using his father's old coffeepot, which he located in the farthest recesses of the cabinet. It took him a few minutes to think through the procedure since at work, where he consumed more than enough caffeine to want it at home, he popped a cartridge into a machine and pressed a button. Marguerite was a tea drinker. He took his lunch to the island and watched the flurries accumulating on the other side of the French doors. Elation getting the best of him, he recorded *grilled cheese sandwich*, *snow*, and *espresso* on three Post-its before taking a bite and sticking them on the dining room wall.

* * *

By the time Marguerite called to him from the mudroom, his mood had mellowed to a notch below contentment.

"How'd it go today?" she asked, filling a kettle with water and setting it on the stove.

"Okay. Really fine."

"You don't sound fine." She dropped a tea bag into a rose-patterned china mug and took a carton of milk from the fridge.

"No, it *was* fine. *Better* than fine. Just feeling a little—"

"Lost again?" He was glad she hadn't said depressed.

"Yeah. You could say that."

"Should I ask the big question?" she said.

"I think you just did. And, yes, I told them."

"How did Gunther take it?" The kettle whistled and she took it off the burner and filled her mug.

"If I'd handed him a ticket to Paris, he couldn't have been happier."

They both laughed.

"He's such a prick," she said. "Glad I won't have to sit next to him at any more holiday parties."

"Want me to take the chairs out of the van?"

"I didn't buy them. They were too far gone. I told you they lie."

"Is there anyone who doesn't?"

"I honestly don't know. The seller said, 'They're antiques! What did you expect?' I think most of the time people rationalize so much they actually believe they're right."

"A truth revealed." He grinned.

"Here's to truth!" She raised her steaming mug.

"To truth," he said, picking up the closest thing to him—a tall green bottle of olive oil. "Want to go out to eat?"

"I picked up Mexican on the way home." She pointed to the plastic bag on the counter. "I just want to stay in with you and Miss Penelope." She scooped up the cat and cradled it in her arms. "I love Miss Penelope, don't you?" She kissed the purring feline's head.

"Of course I do. In fact, why don't we get another pet? A dog. Maybe a German Shepherd or a Great Dane. Or a Saint Bernard. Now that I'll be home to train it."

"Maybe," she said. "It would be an adjustment for Miss Penelope."

"Well, we're all about adjustments at the moment, aren't we?"

"How much of this is about us—me?" she asked, taking a more somber tone. The cat jumped out of her arms and disappeared.

"I'm not sure it's *you* at all. I just can't seem to sustain anything. Something's missing from the mix."

"What mix?" she asked.

"You know—*joie de vivre.*"

After dinner he lit a fire and they sat on the floor, hypnotized by the flames and Miles Davis's *Kind of Blue.*

"Let's go to bed early," he said as the fire died down. That meant: Let's make love before we're too tired.

"Do you really want to?" she asked.

"I suggested it, didn't I?"

In bed they hugged for a while, tenderly stroking each other the same way they might have caressed Miss Penelope—reassuring each other that everything would be okay—before they let their hands roam to more erogenous zones. He kissed her hard, with a kind of desperation, knowing that she'd let him despite any discomfort. They came quickly—she first, then he. After nineteen years together, each knew what turned the other on.

"It's not you," he murmured as they pulled up the covers. He put an arm around her and drew her to him. He loved her as much as— really more than—he had when he first met her on the T in Boston and awkwardly offered her his seat. She'd later told him she'd almost been insulted: she wasn't an old woman, or a weak young one. But she had sensed his genuine desire to become acquainted and was touched by the effort he was making.

When she fell asleep he got out of bed, went down to the kitchen, and wrote *sex* and *Marguerite* on Post-its and put them up on the dining room wall. He wrote *Miss Penelope* and *jazz* on two more, only this time he left the pad on the table. He would buy Marguerite a brand-new package of them—a rainbow assortment.

* * *

In the morning, he persuaded her to drive to their favorite cross-country ski area; the lady in Lenox could wait a little longer for chairs. Their conversation on the ski trails was minimal, and he again relished the silent, natural beauty of the wooded area and the satisfaction of having pushed his body to its limits. On the way home, they stopped at a café for lunch and ordered two bowls of tomato-cheddar soup and a disappointing caprese salad whose hothouse tomatoes were tasteless: "A potato," his father would have called them. The mozzarella was hard and yellow.

"What did you expect this time of year? Heirloom tomatoes from the farmers' market?" Marguerite said.

"I agree about the tomatoes, but you can't slap a leaf of basil on a slab of dry rubber, give it a fancy name, and make it all better. Cheese knows no season. They should do better or not serve it at all." To which she agreed.

Marguerite spent the rest of the afternoon at her computer, searching for Louis XV chairs. She found a pair in Philadelphia from a dealer she trusted. They would need reupholstering, and this meant having to convince the Lenox client to pay for the shipping, labor, and time it would take Marguerite to find a fabric to the woman's liking. It was never as easy as the decorators on the TV home shows made it appear, she complained to Karl. Where were the tears of gratitude when customers saw the final product? She generally encountered outrage over the invoices she tried to keep to a minimum.

Meanwhile, Karl went to the library and took out the novel by the author he'd heard interviewed on the radio, but after giving it thirty pages he grew bored and put it down. When he was ten, his parents had sent him to a summer program in Connecticut for dyslexics, but he still struggled with some of the coping techniques. Fiction had never appealed to him: he preferred to put his energies into journalism, biographies, and other factual works.

That evening he couldn't think of anything he enjoyed that wasn't already displayed on the wall. He entertained the idea of citing activities he disliked, but what would be the point? It would only add to his confusion. Frustrated with having nothing to report, he posted *good food*, underlining *good* three times.

* * *

In the weeks that followed, Karl and Marguerite took salsa dancing lessons, but he couldn't remember the step sequences. He enrolled in cooking classes at a kitchen equipment store and prepared fresh Thai rolls, spicy red lentil soup with sweet potato, and warm pears poached in red wine for Marguerite. He took a series of yoga classes that resulted in back spasms that laid him up for several days. When spring began to show its face in late March, he bought a fancy new bike with an Italian name and took off for apple and peach orchards and freshly manured farmland that was being tilled for the sweet butter-and-sugar corn it would yield.

He was most attracted to dairy farms, where he watched the cows for long periods, deciding they were not as unintelligent as people said they were, and appreciating their ability to offer humans such luscious forms of sustenance. Everything about their laconic nature liberated him. It was as though nothing—neither time nor weather—except preparing to produce was of any relevance to them. Perhaps *this* was how pregnant women felt, *this* was part of that miraculous gestation period. He wouldn't know, and neither would Marguerite. It hadn't been their choice, but it was a situation they accepted. Some days he waited a long time, until one of the animals meandered over to where he straddled his bike on the other side of a stone wall or wire fence and met him face-to-face: "We know, Karl," her eyes said. And he believed she did, and he was grateful to her.

"Remember the annual Wilkshire County Fair?" the cows sometimes asked. As a child he had felt at home in the smelly, muddy barns, turned on by the mooing and the clucking, unbothered by the droppings and torrential pissing. The farmers let children bottle-feed goats and shear sheep, and these were activities he grasped quickly, and with deep pleasure. But to him the fair was solely a place of amusement rather than a glimpse of a potential career. He couldn't remember the last time he'd been to a county fair; the only fairs his parents took him to in his later years were college ones.

* * *

Marguerite was patient about the wall that, by April, was almost completely covered in little yellow pieces of paper. She noticed some duplicates but didn't bring them to Karl's attention. Karl was still dabbling in this or that—happier than he'd been four months earlier but no nearer to making any life-changing decisions. Until one evening, while he was preparing a pizza with packaged mozzarella he had bought at the co-op, she pressed him. "Don't you think it's time, Karl? I mean, to get some direction?"

She was right, of course. He'd been stalling and had come to depend on her to resolve situations: general contracting—that was another career at which she would have excelled. He stayed up most of that night examining his Post-it notes. He laid out on the table those that truly spoke to his heart and proceeded to eliminate the rest, until he was left with *good food, love, family, big animals, nature, grungy work clothes, being own boss*. He further refined the selection: *animals, good food*, and *nature*. He would work outdoors, around animals, with the aim of creating something unique to eat. He would be an entrepreneur. But of what?

He went online, and in the morning had his answer. "I'd like to make mozzarella. *Fresh* mozzarella. Delicious and moist mozzarella that you can't get around here," he said. "I remember cheese like that. I don't know how or where my grandparents got it for their restaurant, but I remember the consistency, the texture—wet but at the same time dry. When you cut into it with your fork, a creamy juice—milk—flowed across the plate. I remember the taste."

With her back to him, Marguerite put a chai tea bag into the china mug and filled it with boiling water, shooed Miss Penelope off the counter, and, unable to stall any longer, turned to face him. He could tell that she didn't know whether to laugh at his intention or cry at his insanity. "And how," she asked, gingerly sitting down and wrapping her hands around the mug she had placed on the island, "did you come to that conclusion?"

Pumped, even after a sleepless night, he explained.

"Karl, couldn't you just make beer like everyone else? I mean, how are we going to make mozzarella?"

"I've been researching. We raise water buffaloes."

"Water buffaloes!" Her eyes widened with amazement.

"Their milk makes the best cheese. The kind you get at the best

Italian trattorias—only better. *They* have it flown in from Italy daily; *we'll* be able to provide it at a savings. Margi, it can go for thirty bucks a pound! We can undersell by cutting out transportation costs."

"I don't know what to say," she said, shaking her head.

"I do feel a bit foolish, having taken all these years to come to this realization."

"I guess the road of life is like any other. Sometimes you have to expect delays."

"This isn't some stalling technique. We can do this, Margi. I *know* we can."

"Where? How?"

"There's a dairy farm for sale in Moulton. One of the farmers told me about it. The owner had plans of turning it into an inn with a wildlife zoo when he retired. It's small—just thirty acres."

"You've been talking to farmers?"

"Yeah. One in particular: Chet Wojcik. I like his cows. I even like *him*." He was describing the chunky, round-faced guy a little older than himself who limited his words to the essential. "Third generation on the farm. When he told me that no question I asked him was a stupid one, I knew we could be friends."

"He raises water buffalo?"

"No! Nobody around here does. That's the point."

"We can't afford to buy now, Karl. You know that."

"I do. But if the owner is willing to lease, we can remortgage this house and rent it out. That gives us enough left to buy the animals and equipment. Maybe we cash in a few bonds. Even set up a Kickstarter page."

"We're not begging for charity. And where's the farmer going?"

"His wife is sick. They're relocating to Arizona to be near their son."

She looked around.

"I know," he said. "You don't like the thought of someone else living here. But it would only be the house—we could move all the furniture, all your treasures."

"They're just things. That's what I tell my clients when they can't decide. I try to put it into perspective. It always lifts them out of their paralysis."

"Right." He was elated with her thought process. "People will say it's a midlife crisis. That we're insane. I don't see it that way. I see it as the beginning of something I've been searching for my whole life. Change is good if we do it together. What else have we got?"

He realized he might regret that last statement.

"Just mozzarella." She pondered the notion, glossing over his words.

"Just mozzarella. We concentrate on one thing. We start small. We make the best available in New England, and then maybe the US."

"Buy American." She laughed, then bit her bottom lip. "You know, when I was little, I dreamed of starting an animal refuge. I still think about it."

"You never told me."

"I thought you'd think I was nuts. But *you're* crazier. In a way, this *is* kind of a refuge."

"Yeah." If that was the way she looked at it, great. "You can still run your business on the side, if you want."

"If I *want*?" she said. "I think I'll *need to* is more like it. In time, who knows? I might find water buffaloes more to my liking. After all, they can't talk back and they have nothing to return."

"Not *any* water buffaloes," he explained. "*River* buffaloes. Look." On his phone he pulled up a photo of a deep chocolate-brown creature with red-tipped facial hairs accentuating the soft, appealing eyes and nose. Horns extended out and curled upward.

"Cute."

"About fifteen hundred pounds of cuteness." He smiled with satisfaction. "The ones in the States are docile, scared of their shadows. They were originally used to cut down on the weed problem, then for meat. Now they're pets that behave like cows. I like cows. They mind their own business."

* * *

Karl continued to visit online sites and also read all the agrarian books he could find. He spent time with Chet, who introduced him to other dairy farmers. They all cautioned him about the cost of maintaining buffalo in the New England climate, particularly if his intent was to derive income solely from cheese—and *one* kind of cheese at that. But once an idea had been planted in his head, Karl became driven.

Next, he embarked on an odyssey that began with a one-way flight to Rome. From there he drove to a small mozzarella factory near Mondragone, about twenty-five miles from Naples, where two brothers continued the family tradition of using only buffalo milk, while other factories had begun to mix in milk from cows. Staying at an *agriturismo* in the same town, Karl showed up at the factory every morning. The men communicated through the brothers' few words of English, Karl's few of household Italian, a dictionary, many hand gestures, and a lot of realia, which worked to Karl's advantage, since it was through observation and hands-on experience that he learned best. To Karl's relief, the brothers were more than willing to reveal the secrets of their art. They were, in fact, proud to demonstrate their expertise and equally generous with their hospitality, inviting him to the afternoon *pranzo* their wives prepared. Truth be told, Karl sensed the Italians' opinion that this naïve American could never re-create as excellent a product as their own.

In a rudimentary facility akin to a three-walled barn, the stocky Lorenzo—wearing a sleeveless T-shirt, long black apron, and a cheesecloth cap over his black hair—added a natural coagulant to the giant wooden vat of buffalo milk. Before long the brothers' bare hands were wrist-deep in the mixture, breaking up into small pieces the curds the coagulant had formed. Next, Franco poured boiling water over the pieces to melt them and allow them to blend as the men stirred—four hairy arms and a paddle in continuous circular motion—relying on their many years of experience to tell them when the mixture approached the proper consistency: it should be stringy and rubbery but not tough. After it had partly cooled, it was ready to be formed into balls that when cut exuded whey and gave off an aroma that drew Karl to the cheese like he were an infant finding the teat.

Would latex gloves interfere with the taste? Did the vat have to be wooden? Surely, in the States I will be required to use stainless steel, Karl thought as the balls were cooled in salted water before they were wrapped in waxed paper for shipment to market. He filmed the process and offered to pay the brothers, but they wanted no part of it. "Tell everyone in America who it was that taught you," they said, confident that it would take Karl a century to become adept at the process.

The brothers directed Karl to the dairy farmers who sold them their milk, and they taught Karl the best way to milk a water buffalo. He carefully observed their pasteurization method—a process during which, Chet had told him, pH-related issues could go awry, affecting a product's flavor. They promised to send him their buffalo semen to artificially inseminate his herd: if they were going to give milk, they would need to be lactating; and if they were going to be lactating, they would need to produce calves all the time. From Italy he flew to Canada and interned for two weeks on a ranch in eastern Ontario.

In his absence, Marguerite held a yard sale, carted boxes of books and clothes to Goodwill, and sold on Craigslist larger items she could live without. "It felt good to pare down," she said when he returned, sure of himself. If she had doubts about their life-changing decision, she kept them to herself. They found a young university adjunct and his wife to move into their home in September.

"They might have children," Karl said. "Children make messes."

"Messes can be cleaned up," she said. "Anything can be repaired." And then later as they lay awake, unable to quiet their exhausted yet excited bodies: "It's happening."

"Yeah," he said, feeling an erection coming on.

* * *

Marguerite found the interior of the narrow farmhouse—rooms that had been added on one behind the other at different times in

its history—in only slightly better shape than the exterior of weathered clapboards in desperate need of painting. For now, she chose
to redo the two rooms that would provide sanctuary and sanity: the
bedroom, which she painted eggplant—her favorite paint company's color of the year—and the four-season porch in the rear, which
would serve as her office and which she decorated in gray tones with
black accents to complement her salmon oriental rug and the black
combination desk and bookcase (or *home office ensemble*, as it was
known in the trade). Marguerite's income, though unpredictable,
seemed to ease her apprehension, but the meditation fountain she
purchased for the corner of her new office belied her exterior bravado. She would give it a year, she told Karl; then they'd reevaluate.

Karl's unbridled energy lent itself well to a farmer's schedule.
He cleaned and prepared his stalls as though he were running a
B and B for buffalo. He purchased giant round bales of hay that
were wrapped in white plastic to withstand the elements, and that,
stacked in the fields, resembled marshmallows on steroids.

On a crisp September morning he rose before dawn to inseminate the first of six buffaloes that had been delivered by a Louisiana
rancher. The semen from Italy would guarantee him at least a
part-Italian buffalo. Besides, Chet had warned him about the dan-
gers of using bulls for insemination. "The only bull that's gonna
hurt you is the one you give the chance to."

The first buffalo he would attempt to inseminate was the one
that was already standing. Karl patted her on the head. That was
all, but it was enough. The animal let out a bark that continued as
she chased him out of the barn and all the way to the fence Karl
managed to hurl his body over. While Karl disappeared behind a
sugar maple, the frenzied animal charged in a straight line, breaking
through the split-rail fence and carrying a piece of it on her horns
all the way to the road, where a tractor-trailer ran over her.

"I thought you said they were docile!" Marguerite shouted,
breathing heavily. She had run outside when she heard the screeching and commotion. Her white terry-cloth robe fell open below her
waist and flapped around her long, tanned legs, leaving nothing to

the imagination. Karl stood in shock as the truck driver, though apologetic, took it all—including Marguerite—in. It was tragic—a financial blow too, he understood—but not unusual in his world. "Animals are unpredictable," the driver said, surmising that Karl was a newcomer to husbandry. "Happens." He tied the carcass to the back of his trailer and dragged it close to the field. "Just leave her in the wild like they do out west. Vultures will get to her fast enough. Be gone in no time. Less you wanna dig a grave. I'd help you, but I'm already behind schedule. Gotta be in Birmingham tomorrow." And with that he hopped in the cab of his semi and took off.

Having no idea about the protocol for disposing of dead cattle, Karl called Chet, who assured him that as soon as he finished milking, he'd come by and haul the dead animal to a remote field on his own property. "We don't bury anymore: it'd contaminate the groundwater, or so they say. And we sure as hell don't leave 'em out to rot. Might have done that thirty, forty years ago, but we don't have those kinds of open spaces anymore. Compost is the right way to do it. And I told you, a single-strand electric fence is the only way to keep them off the road—unless you get a short or you leave the damn gate open. The road's their worst enemy."

"They must feel like children given up for adoption," Karl said to Marguerite over the cup of black coffee she brought out to him. She had offered to fix him breakfast, but he was too nauseated to down anything else. "How could I be so stupid? They aren't going to behave the way the ones in Canada did."

"Maybe they're not ready to be inseminated."

"They're ready." Karl was adamant as he sized up the broken fence he would have to repair quickly. "I've seen their discharge, and one of them tried to mount another yesterday. They're ready. We've got to breed them by October or in winter their udders will get congested from cold and frost. If we're successful, we give them another dry period just like they've been in for the last two months—we don't milk until we breed again in June. Gives them a chance to build up their reserves."

Impressed with his knowledge, she asked, "And what's with the barking noise?"

"That's what they do. They don't moo," a despondent Karl said, lugging another piece of broken fence to the pile he was making.

"And here I thought they were just happy as clams. I guess they've been in shock. At least Miss Runaway Bride was." The identity Marguerite gave the animal made Karl chuckle despite his despair. "We *are* going to have to name them, you know, Karl. How else can we talk about them—or *to* them?"

He hadn't thought about that. Of course, they'd have to name them; they were as much a part of the family now as Miss Penelope. They walked back to the barn and found the remaining five buffalo out grazing in the field.

"They're unfazed. Maybe they didn't like her," Marguerite said.

"Maybe they're just hungry."

"Let's call the one with the spiky hair Cyndi Lauper," Marguerite said.

"Well, if she's Cyndi, how about Lady Gaga for the one lying down, sunning herself? She looks pretty privileged. And Gladys Knight for her"—Karl pointed to one with sleek black hair and piercing eyes. "She looks smart, and kind of sexy."

"The one with the white streak down the center of her head is definitely Tina Turner."

"And the one that keeps looking at you as though you should have known better?" Marguerite asked.

"Adele."

"It's a significant setback before we've even started," Karl said.

Marguerite nodded. At least she was honest.

* * *

The next morning, he tried again with Lady Gaga, who had been the first to come into the barn after grazing. "They won't stay out long in winter," Chet had said. "Especially when the wind picks up. They don't like wind." He was more careful this time to woo his coy mistress, talking to her for quite some time while staring directly into her big glistening eyes: How did she like her new digs? Wasn't she looking smashing on this blustery morning? Every statement was followed with a generous smile. And then came the mellow half vocal, half humming serenade of "Brown Eyed Girl." Only then did he attempt the human touch, and by this time Lady Gaga was more than ready for it. Starting at her head, he ran his palm over her warm, smooth coat, tracing her spine the same way he petted Miss Penelope—and Marguerite. By the time he ventured to insert the syringe, Lady Gaga accepted the intrusion without protest. And so it went with Tina, Gladys, Adele, and Cyndi, accomplishing the feat without even having to secure the animals in the stanchion most farmers used for milking.

There was much to be done during the gestation period that would carry them through winter and into spring. Karl still hadn't secured the funds to set up a pasteurization operation. He could have sent his raw milk out to a larger dairy, the way Chet did, but he didn't trust commercial processing and feared it might alter the taste of the perfect cheese he aspired to produce. Then an angel materialized out of cyberspace, an angel about whom Karl had received a heads-up from the receptionist of Western Mass Wealth Management. He was a venture capitalist from Sweden who also had a farming fantasy, coupled with good business sense and a wagonload of cash; a man who secretly envisioned himself and Karl as the new Ben and Jerry. When Karl confirmed that he wasn't interested in making anything but mozzarella, the silent partner agreed, planning to remain silent for as long as he saw it was fiscally advantageous to do so.

With this new source of capital, Karl ordered five more water buffalo. He hired a carpenter to build a heated cement-floor shed with plumbing and purchased state-of-the-art pasteurization equipment. Meanwhile, Marguerite expanded and redesigned the milking barn, creating roomier stalls and adding soundproofing. Her goal was to create a mellow, churchlike atmosphere where the "moms and babies" would feel happy, peaceful, and comfortable.

She renamed it "the nursery". There would be no noise within, and no sounds of machinery or farm work without. This would be their time—mom time.

"Why not?" she said to Karl. "If it works for humans, it can work for buffaloes."

How did she know all this? he inquired. She had worked with enough pregnant women and new moms, she said. If she could have gotten the animals into rocking chairs, she would have. She was becoming as attached to the expectant mothers she visited before and after work—and they to her—as if she were vicariously carrying the calves. Even Miss Penelope overcame her initial jealousy to become a frequent and familiar visitor to the barn of freestalls, where the buffalo were allowed to come and go as they pleased and where the cat, curled up against the buffaloes' warm, swollen bellies, napped.

When Chet told Karl he needed to purchase hutches—plastic-domed huts that looked like oversized doghouses for the pasture—so the calves would be able to get in and out of weather fast, Karl entertained the notion. They came in multiple sizes—small for a single calf, larger for two, and even bigger for several—and would be useful until the calves were integrated into the adult system. This concept, however, horrified Marguerite, who insisted that the calves remain with their mothers. She went so far as to liken Karl's behavior to that of their cruel and devious president, who separated immigrant children from their parents at the border.

In midsummer, Karl hired a helper with a tractor and chopper to harvest the corn the former landowners had sown. The worker ground up the whole plant—leaves, stalk, and ears—and stored it in the farm's small silos. This left Karl free to take pleasure in observing his children, as he and Marguerite had begun to call the buffalo, as they wandered from stall to feedbox, from water trough to grazing field.

* * *

Two years passed. Marguerite cried when they sold their home to the professor, who had secured a tenure-track position, in order to purchase more buffalo, a new pickup, and a combine. As consolation, she remodeled the kitchen of the property they could not afford to buy and decorated the rest of the rooms, into which she moved the remainder of their furniture. With Karl promising impending success, they dined out often—driving to Worcester, Boston, and Providence—frequenting high-end trattorias and talking up their endeavor to hungry restaurateurs they befriended and who begged for a date when the coveted cheese could be expected.

They found a full-time farmhand, a lanky but strong, prematurely balding eighteen-year-old named Ben, fresh out of a vocational high school that boasted a strong agricultural program. He was a chatterbox, and Karl feared Ben would disturb the buffaloes, but the boy was skilled at milking, harvesting, and planting, and meticulous at cleaning out the stalls each morning, clipping long hair around udders, and hosing down the ladies when it was hot. Like Marguerite and Karl, he thrilled to the birth of each calf, but unlike them, he was a professional who did not mourn the selling of each male. That's how Karl knew early on that Ben was destined for a grander enterprise.

Karl and Ben found that the ladies gave a lot more milk when their calves were nearby, and so at 5 a.m. each morning they brought the babies in from pasture to their mothers, who licked the calves and gave off grunts that Karl was sure meant, "I love you." While Marguerite referred to the milking barn as the nursery, Karl likened it to the comfort of a family kitchen, where strategies for letting down their milk—like recipes—were passed from generation to generation. He swore that when the buffalo who had been in the milking barn as calves became moms for the first time, giving milk was a breeze: they had already seen it done.

But if Ben and Karl sensed that the moms were feeling nervous, the men couldn't get a drop of milk during the four-hour milking period, and for that reason Marguerite insisted it wasn't just a matter of what the new moms had observed as calves: they needed to be in a relaxed atmosphere so their pituitary glands could produce oxytocin, a hormone that created feelings of bonding, love, and trust. In a sense, both sides were right, because despite their different takes, of one thing they could be sure: when the love was flowing, so was the milk.

* * *

Milk is measured in pounds: first they got six, then twelve, and eventually the eighteen Karl felt they needed to attempt to make mozzarella. At first he made micro test batches, stirring until he got enough elasticity to form balls whose shape was close to what he had seen in Italy and remembered from his childhood, but it was never to his liking. Frustrated, he tried over and over to get it right—perfect—until, from a handful of cheese, he squeezed out a smooth, slippery, glistening ball. Months passed. "*E quando?*" The restaurateurs pleaded for a timeline. When he was confident enough of the flavor and consistency, he took samples to several of them, who found it close enough to what they were importing and more cost effective, and who then placed orders.

But it was too late. Clients aren't the only ones with demands: investors also want results, and after four years, his Scandinavian partner broke his silence. He sent his investment manager—a young blond and blue-eyed man named Lucas Nilsson, whose DNA might have been a good match for Marguerite's, so similar were their features.

"This is all very good. *Ja.* Very nice, Mr. Siracconi," Lucas said. His exceptionally deep voice contrasted with his youthful appearance as he carefully stepped around the puddles caused by the recent thaw. He winced when his Italian leather slip-ons sank into mud. He examined the orderly stalls.

"Please, call me Karl."

Lucas nodded in approval of the neatly stacked white rolls of hay. His awkward chuckle when Karl introduced each animal by name seemed to stem less from finding the personification endearing and more from the fear that Karl might be expecting him to shake each buffalo's hoof.

Later, sitting in one of matching red-and-blue floral wing chairs of the granite-colored living room, Lucas appeared at ease. His unzipped gray windbreaker revealed a blue-striped shirt and red paisley tie. Seated on the sofa across from him, Karl could not help but notice how well Lucas fit in with the décor. Marguerite, who placed a tray of tea and biscuits on the iron-framed glass coffee table, must have found him appealing.

"As I said earlier, Mr. Siracconi—Karl—this is all very nice, but the bottom line is, we need to be making money."

"We will—we *are*." Karl was indignant.

"Karl, it's been four years and you have yet to turn a profit—at least, one to speak of. And you will *not*, according to our calculations, without expanding your product line. At least add several buffalo milk products—burrata, ricotta, yogurt." When Lucas persisted, Karl refused, a look of hurt and incomprehension on his face.

"We'll think about it," Marguerite said, pouring Lucas a second cup of tea. "Can you give us until the end of this week?"

Karl glared at her.

"Let's talk on Friday." He removed a card from his wallet and placed it on the table.

"Can we email you?"

"I prefer a call, Mrs. Siracconi." She resisted the urge to tell him she had a different surname. Taking in the orderly surroundings, he asked, "Do you have any children?"

"We have thirty-six, Mr. Nilsson," Marguerite responded pointedly.

*   *   *

"Maybe he's right, Karl," Marguerite said after spitting a mouthful of toothpaste into the bathroom sink. "Ben gave notice. We'll never get another hand like him for the same pay." She quickly wrung out a hot washcloth and placed it over her face to hide the disgusted expression he knew was about to appear on it.

"Absolutely not!" he said, bellowing. The toilet he flushed roared in agreement.

"What's the harm?" she said beneath the steaming cloth. But he knew she knew the answer: he would not—could not—reverse course. He was incapable of redirecting his mind once it was made up. Even Ben must have seen the writing on the wall. Poor Karl, she was probably thinking. Poor fucking, stubborn Karl.

They both knew how it would play out from here. He would rant for a while each night that week, hit the pillow with his fist several times, pretending it was Lucas Nilsson's face, and then (crying "Fuck *me!*") sink into sulking mode—or worse. How far could he push love—Marguerite's for him, his for the buffalo—to follow a dream? Before the sun had risen on Friday, she answered one of those questions. If he didn't take the investor's advice, they should separate. Hearing that, he took off on the long drive to hike Mount Monadnock.

He returned at five to find a note on the kitchen table: *Please stop balling up the dishtowel after you use it. Fold it and place it over the oven handle to dry.* The words pissed him off so much he almost didn't bother to read the rest of the note: *And please come to the barn.* Yes, he knew he was late and hadn't seen to it that the feedboxes were full, if that was all she was insinuating. But he put nothing past her, and with trepidation about something greater than a scolding, headed out to the barn.

Bewilderment compounded his anxiety when he found a folding table and chairs set with Marguerite's favorite French-print cloth and napkins, two white-and-gold china plates, a pair of her mother's Waterford crystal wine goblets that hadn't made their way out of the china cabinet since the woman's death—and the buffaloes, looking well fed and content in their stalls.

"You could have dressed," she said, eyeing his red-and-white plaid flannel shirt, faded jeans, and linty fleece vest. She proceeded to light two white tapers in brass holders. "I wore my best Wellies." She gestured toward the high black rubber boots pulled over a pair of black velvet pants topped with a white satin blouse.

"At least I wore black," he said, looking down at his vest.

"I hope you like Chinese."

Of course, he liked Chinese. He sat in front of a plate of his favorite takeout, chao fan noodles with shrimp, and poured them each a glass of the pinot noir nestled in a silver holder.

"What are you eating?" he asked.

"Salt-and-pepper tofu with akai rice. We can share." She always ordered akai rice when she needed to settle her stomach.

"What's this about, Margi?" he asked, still feeling he was treading on shaky ground. "A farewell dinner? A last supper of sorts?"

"More like a family meeting." She smiled, taking in the contented buffaloes.

"I haven't called him yet, and I probably won't today. It's almost midnight in Sweden." He was not apologetic.

"Did you hear that, ladies? He *still* hasn't called! What do you say?" The docile animals stared back at her. "That's what I thought. It's unanimous," she said. "We stay the course."

* * *

If the Swedish investor hadn't pulled out, the story might have been different, or at least part of it would have. Mozzarella was secondary to the investor, who took the entire pasteurization setup he had paid for to California, where he established a plant that made buffalo milk ice cream. Karl's business too would have succeeded with other products, but Karl was intent on holding on to his dream, on capturing that taste and texture—that something from his past. When Ben left in the summer to work on a much larger farm, Marguerite rose alongside Karl to help with the early morning chores. Despite dipping into their meager savings and selling off some of their beloved livestock, they could never accrue enough money to hire proper help or build an adequate new pasteurization facility of their own. Nevertheless, whether Karl had figured out the process or not, it was always going to be his way. The next year, he was convinced, would always be better.

One night, as Karl listened to the buzzing of cicadas while lying beside Gladys Knight—his head resting on a mound of hay and her enormous ear butting up against his torso—Karl told her all that. Refusing defeat, exhausted yet satisfied with what he had accomplished, he relayed what they were on the cusp of achieving. She cast her eyes upward toward his face. Staring at the rafters, he did not see them—sad, wise, and wet—as with optimism, he persisted in assuring her, and himself, of a long and lucrative future.

She, however, attuned to his inner workings, listened to other plans, plans being laid out by an unwanted guest: a new silent partner who, unbeknown to Karl, had taken up residence in his pancreas, where it plotted day and night the sinister outcome of its own ambitions.

The Sound of Your Voice

"I'm so glad you called," Jeannette says, the receiver nestled between her shoulder and her ear while she sweeps breakfast crumbs off the kitchen counter. "It's a good time. *He's* gone to the post office."

"The daughter of our pilot, Chuck McCarthy, wrote to me," Fred says. "The girl's looking for a photo of her father with the crew of the *Laurie Belle*—the plane we named after her—and copies of old orders, any kind of remembrance. Poor thing never knew him."

"After all this time?"

"How much time has it been?"

"Over fifty years since the war ended. The big one—our war, that is. She's hardly a little girl anymore, Fred."

"What's time at this point?" He states this more than asks.

"Do you have anything?"

"One of the crew in front of the plane. They'd just returned from a mission that was recalled due to bad weather. I wasn't in it."

"Why not?"

"Bad ear infection. Grounded for one week."

"I don't remember that."

"I must have written you about it."

"You know I burned almost all your letters," she says matter-of-factly. "Does it hurt you to hear that?"

"Not anymore."

"I've never heard you mention Ron Taylor."

"Didn't fly with us. He's chairman of the 453rd Bomber Group for *the Second Air Division Association of the Eighth Air Force Newsletter*. Ain't that a mouthful! Lives in Rolla, Missouri, now. Sent out letters to all the members of the 735th BS, Crew Sixty-Eight."

"BS?" She laughs.

"Bomb Squad."

"Of course. Forgive me," she says, assuming a proper English accent.

"Sophomoric humor was never a trait of yours, Jeannette."

"I was too serious."

"I thought you said *I* was too serious."

"You were. And I didn't help you to be otherwise. But before you, I'd never been in love with anyone except dead poets and Cary Grant. You remind me of him."

"Browning or Frost?"

"No, silly. Grant."

"I'm much taller."

"Are you?"

"Hell yes! Even now. We should be more profane," he says, insistent.

"Agreed."

"Yes. Fuck anyone who doesn't like it."

"How about we just plain fuck?" Jeannette says.

"Yes! Let's, my darling little harlot! That was our biggest mistake: we didn't fuck enough. In fact, we didn't fuck at all."

"Cary Grant fucked a lot of women: Grace Kelly, Sophia Loren, Eva Marie Saint."

"I don't know if he fucked Eva Marie Saint."

"Well, he was about to on the train in *North by Northwest*. Nowadays they'd have gone all the way on the screen."

"I kind of liked it when they left something to the imagination."

"I kind of like watching the fucking scenes. I even like watching wo—"

"What? What were you going to say?" Fred is eager to know.

"Never mind."

"Not *that* liberated? You know you can tell me anything, Jeannette. In fact, you don't even have to tell me. At this point, I already know; I can see your thoughts tumbling ahead of your words."

"So why do I bother telling you anything, smarty-pants?"

"Because you need to. Because you know I love to hear your voice. Tell me something: Do you ever feel you were born on the wrong side of time?"

"I regret not being brave enough to change the course of time. Fuck! It's getting late. Gotta run."

"Felt good, didn't it?" he asks before she hangs up.

"What?" she asks.

"To say that. We guys said it and a lot worse overseas all the time."

"Fuck! Fuck! Fuck! Yes! It feels damn good."

* * *

"Hello, sweetheart, are you free to talk?" Fred is upbeat.

"I still have that—you know—the blue silk handkerchief with *Sweetheart* and air force wings embroidered on it that you sent me from Scotland." Jeannette barely speaks above a whisper.

"When I was on furlough," he says in confirmation. "More like a mandated R and R to calm my nerves. Sent my mother one, too. Not with *Sweetheart* on it, of course, but *Mother*."

"Must have made her happy."

"Nothing made her happy."

"Your family *was* a sullen group," she says, whispering.

"Doesn't sound like you're free to talk."

"No. How about you write?"

"I'm not as poetic as I used to be."

"No need to be. Just write. Anything you say will be more welcome than the gibberish of the younger generation. It pains me that good grammar has gone out the window. Please write. I so loved your letters."

"Do you do email?" Fred asks.

"No. I don't even have a computer! Do you?"

"Of course," he says with pride. "You must have a cell phone."

"My, my, you're really *with it*."

"If you don't have a computer, how do you read the gibberish emails of the young?"

"I don't. My grandchildren send me cards now and then. I take a red pen and make corrections."

"Jeannette, I hope you don't send them back to them."

"Of course I do. But I also draw hearts and tell them I love them all the same."

"That's harsh, *grandma*."

"That's an English teacher for you, I guess."

"I'm so proud of you."

"You just said it was harsh."

"I mean: going to college when your children were grown, getting a degree, becoming a teacher."

"I loved teaching. Wish I had never retired."

"What's that in the background?"

"The radio. The *Music of Our Time* station."

"But what song?" he asks.

"'Fly Me to the Moon.'"

"That's fitting."

"Will you?" she asks.

"Will I what?"

"Fly me there?"

"And back again."

"No. Not back. Shall I make it louder, Fred?"

"Just stay on until the end."

"If you-know-who comes into the room, I'll have to hang up."

"I can call you on your cell phone when you're out of the house."

"We only have one that we save for emergency calls."

"Well, give me the number."

"I can't. *He* carries it in his pocket all the time."

"You can use a pay phone the way you did when we first started to talk."

"The one by the supermarket is gone."

"Find another."

"They're going as we speak. By the next time we talk, they'll all be gone."

* * *

"Do you remember our last date before I shipped out? I was home on furlough from Fort Bragg. Our crew had just picked up our plane in San Francisco and delivered it to Florida. We had gotten our assignments too: pilot—that was McCarthy—copilot, navigator, bombardier, and we had six gunners—me being the ball gunner. I puked on our first practice flight."

She doesn't want to think of him riding alone in the goddamn capsule beneath the belly of the plane and steers the conversation back to their date. "Roosevelt's Ice Cream Parlor on the avenue. Just after we had taken those dreadful photos at the studio. What was the photographer's name?"

"Mr. Bienvenue," he says.

She cracks up, laughing. "Yes. That was it!"

"You looked stunning in that purple-and-green dress with the grape whatever you call them on it."

"Appliqués."

"And your sister's string of fake pearls."

"And my nineteen-forties pompadour hairstyle! And you: cool and calm in your olive-drab jacket with the military pins on the lapels, stripes on the shoulders, khaki tie tucked into your shirt."

"You shut your eyes the way you always did in front of a flash and bright lights. My smile was too big and toothy."

"We didn't look real!" She is still laughing.

"That crazy photographer had twisted our bodies into a most unrealistic and uncomfortable cheek-to-cheek pose. My neck was killing me."

"We always hid our discomfort well."

"Too well," he says with a sigh.

"You know what they say about hindsight."

"Can we blame all our shortcomings on youth?"

"Why not? Damn youth!"

"I still have the wallet size of that photo." He's upbeat again. "Tucked right into the inside pocket of my jacket."

"Do you always wear a jacket, Mr. Saturday Night? I would think you don't get around much anymore."

"Actually, I do."

"Where do you go?"

"Everywhere. But sometimes it's in the pocket of my bathrobe or my shirt."

"And you carried it around—even when *She* was still living?"

"I did. I think *She* knew, but I didn't care."

Jeannette doesn't tell him that she never burned the eight-by-ten portrait—just the letters. Hid it from *Him* for so many years. She loved the broad grin that tapered toward the chin, the straight line of his nose.

"I wanted to get married that night," she says. "But you turned me down."

"I didn't even know where I'd be in two days. You deserved better than that."

"That was an excuse."

"Maybe so. I was only eighteen."

"You got to second base that night in the vestibule of my parents' apartment house."

"I *did?*" He feigns innocence.

"Isn't that what guys called touching a girl's breast? Slipping your hand inside the neckline of my dress until you reached flesh— my nipple! Isn't that what they called it?"

"Yeah," he says, chuckling. "I wonder if they still do."

* * *

"You didn't answer the last few times." Fred's worry is palpable.

"I've been busy with family matters. My grandson got married."

"Already? I thought you said he was fourteen."

"That was awhile back."

"No. It was the last time we spoke."

"Maybe. But time has a way of running off like that, especially at our age. He's twenty-nine."

"I had a dream last night," he says.

"Do you still dream?"

"Of course. Don't you?"

"I hardly sleep."

"I dreamed about Rickels again, the top turret gunner and first engineer. He was older than the rest of us, maybe twenty-five. He and McCarthy were the only ones with kids. We were on the flight from Florida to Puerto Rico, where we had a layover for Christmas Day before heading closer to our unknown destination.

"I got up and walked toward the back of the plane. Rickels looked frozen: his eyes open, staring coldly into space, his facial muscles tensed, nostrils wide. He looked up at me but he didn't speak, as though he was trying hard to contain some hideous secret. I didn't say anything. None of us ever asked questions. But I felt I had to respond somehow, so I stuck my hand into my shirt pocket and offered him a stick of Tutti Frutti gum. I remember it was Tutti Frutti. Rickels turned away with a disgusted look on his face that told me I knew nothing of what he was about. He was right. I knew nothing, just that we were heading for unknown adventures that might keep us away from the good old USA and that might bring heartache and disaster to our loved ones back home, but sorrow was only a notion. Our thoughts weren't of death and disaster but of *new lands* we would see. Would they be the tropics of the Pacific or India? The legendary fogs of London? The honorable sons of heaven or the supermen of the führer? What audacity! How naïve!

"Then McCarthy opened the envelope and passed out the orders. Old Buckingham was to be our humble home for the next six months. The Germans were good fighters; the flak would be thick and accurate, but we consoled ourselves with the thought that at least we wouldn't have to put up with the tropical diseases and scorching climate of the Pacific or Far East. But Rickels knew better. He and McCarthy always knew.

"Later, while we filled our stomachs with Puerto Rican hospitality and rum, and drunkenly sang 'Silent Night' and 'O Come All Ye Faithful,' I fought the lump in my throat and my thoughts of home, I fought what Rickels fought every second. I wish to hell I could have understood him then."

"Did he make it?" Jeannette asks.

"Got court-martialed for refusing to get into the ball turret on the nineteenth mission. They wanted to give him the death sentence, but our squadron CO got him off with fifteen years. One day McCarthy took a mission with another squadron. Went down. But that you already know—from Ron Taylor's letter."

"I wish you'd told me these things when you came home. It would have explained a lot."

"I wasn't a big talker before. I never talked when I came back."

"You came back different, Freddie. I could have helped."

"No, you couldn't have. *I* was different, but *you* weren't. At least you were wise enough to recognize that. Most chose not to."

"But you're good *now*." She more informs him than asks.

"Only now. Tell me about your grandson. What does he do?"

"He's a lawyer. He has two children."

"But he just got married!"

"I told you. Time passes quickly at our age. You shouldn't change the subject."

"Which?"

"About Rickels—the war."

"I'm not changing the subject. Not anymore. I can be in two places at one time. Even more."

"So you're a multitasker."

"Yeah. I suppose."

"I'm sorry." She sighs.

"For what?"

"For not waiting for you."

"But you did."

"Only my body. My mind never understood. My heart collapsed."

There is silence.

"That's why you turned down the ring I tried to give you. Wouldn't even try it on for size."

"And you're still carrying your anger," she says.

"Yes."

"Good. I deserve it."

"No! No, Jeannette! You still don't understand. Not about the then. Not about the now."

"Will you wait for me—until I'm free?" she asks.

"Yes, my love. I will wait for you."

"The years have taken their toll: the Mediterranean salad dressing wasn't all it was cracked up to be. I'd give anything to have had a tube of sunscreen instead of my oil and vinegar concoction. Burn and peel. I thought it was cleansing. Too late now."

"Jesus!" he yells again with frustration, then softens his tone. "Don't you see? It doesn't matter. You are what you've always been to me. Before you go, tell me something: Why did you marry *Him*?"

"Because you married *Her*."

"Only after you married *Him*."

* * *

"'Forty suit, medium shoes, nine glove, and large boots,' I say first thing in the morning, just as I told the fellow behind the counter on thirty-five mornings worlds and eons ago, hoping I've gotten there early enough before they ran out of my sizes."

"Surely you don't still go through this every morning." Jeannette is incredulous.

"Every morning. After all these years. Still living from one day to the next. Anxious to get the fighting over, to know there won't be any more mornings when I wake up dreading the expected call from the CO who's come to say, 'Crew Sixty-Eight? Up and at it, fellows. Looks like a long hop; planes are loaded with twenty-seven

hundred gallons of gas.' I try to squeeze in a few extra minutes of
the comfort of my warm bed, but one by one we all rise to get to
the briefing room before they run out of our sizes. I can hear them.
I can see them, dead or alive. Like the others, I ride my bike or walk
to the mess hall for my fresh or powdered eggs, but it's mostly just
pancakes. I'm never very hungry at three-thirty a.m. None of us are,
but we take a few bites and gulp down some hot coffee to warm up
a bit; the day is so cold, yet it's nothing compared to the temperatures we're about to fly in."

"Then what?" Jeannette asks.

"First thing I do in the briefing room is check the circuit of my
heated equipment with my flashlight: unscrew the back of my light
and then complete the circuit with the plug of the heated equipment. If all's in order, I begin dressing: the heated suit going over
my long johns, followed by the heated shoes, summer flying suit,
scarf, field jacket, leather boots, flying helmet, parachute harness,
life preserver, and heated gloves. Dressing all completed, I drag
myself into the briefing room, sit down, smoke, and wait to see
what the target is, all the while my stomach feeling as though it's
had a double dose of ex-lax. Roll by the intelligence officer. Plane
assignments and the hardstands."

"The *what*?"

"The pavement they're parked on. Then the camera assignments. Finally he reveals the target, the route, the amount of flak
we'll encounter, fighter support—and opposition; ETA at enemy
coast, at target, back to home base. Moans and groans from everyone when the target is a long distance away or one known for heavy
flak from super fighters in places like Brunswick, Berlin, Hamburg,
or any of those big German cities. Cold. It's so cold. Even now I
can feel the cold."

"Still greater than the northeastern cold?"

"Still greater than the coldest of colds."

"But surely by now you know the end did come, that you are no
longer living from one day to the next. You said so yourself—that
you're good now. You can't relive this every morning."

"Every morning," he replies. "What we didn't know then was that we could never erase the past. Am I good? In a sense. But as I've said—different. Still different."

"What happens next? I'm sorry I never asked before."

"I don't think I would have told you. We walk out to the waiting trucks, pile on our equipment, and head out to our ships. We're always greeted heartily by our ground crewmen, a swell bunch of fellows who do their darned best to keep the planes in good shape for us."

She giggles.

"What's funny?" He's confused.

"I'm sorry. But you said 'swell.' It's been so long since I've heard anyone use that expression."

"When I'm there, nothing changes. Everything is as it always was."

"I understand. Really. I'm sorry."

"Stop saying you're sorry! Pity never healed a wound!"

She takes a deep breath and speaks slowly. "I have to tell you that one of the things I've always hated about my husband is that he never apologizes."

"Well, then, apology accepted," he says.

"What happens next?"

"Do you really want to know all this?"

"Freddie, darling, don't you think it's about time?"

"Our main concern is to check our turrets and guns on the ship: then, systematically, the ammunition, oxygen supply, chaff, bomb load, engines, generators, the whole ship in general. Checking the bomb load at the bottom of the fuselage is my job. I've got to see that the safety pins are secure in the fuses and that the load is ready for takeoff. With the ship done, we make sure we have all our equipment, including the extension cords for our heated equipment and our flak suits. And then, my darling, we relax until engine time, when we pile into the ship, the ground crew wishing us luck as we taxi. From the minute we take off to the minute we land, we're on alert. It takes about two hours for each plane in the squadron to climb to high altitude and get into formation. At about five thousand feet, I make my way down to the bomb bay to remove the pins from the fuses. There's a lot of talking between the pilot and navigator going on that can be heard over the interphone: fighter planes are called off by the clock system; flak much the same, except we try and locate the gun positions on the ground. Everything is quiet on the bombing run. We're tense waiting for the bomb bay doors to open properly and the bombardier to say 'Bombs away.' Once over the Channel again, we're a bit relaxed. Are you still there? Still listening? Or have I bored you to death?"

"Still here, my love. Tell me more."

"The ships reach our home base, circle a few times, and land. The solid ground feels good again after eight hours in the air. Everyone is anxious: the ground crew can't wait to ask if we had any trouble with the ship, any wounded; we crewmen want to see where our ship was hit by flak. Sometimes we find a lot of holes; sometimes a few; rarely do we not find any. Trucks take us back to the interrogation room, where we undress and Red Cross workers greet us with hot coffee, sandwiches, and sometimes donuts. That feels so good! It's over. We made it. But the intelligence officer is hankering to know how our bombing went: where the flak areas are, their intensity; fighter opposition; fighter escort; which bombers in our squadron were actually shot down like enemy fighters claimed, or just ditched in the Channel; and on and on. Interrogation over, all we want to do is get back to the barracks and wash up, read our mail, write some letters, and then get to bed early for possibly another mission in the morning. And that, my love, is a good mission, a good day."

"What about the bad ones?"

"I live them too. There were thirty-five missions that can't be separated or parsed in any way, two hundred and forty men who can never become indistinct—forgotten."

"I have to go now, Fred. *He* has a doctor's appointment."

"Serious?"

"Could be."

"I wonder …"

"What?"

"Where you are when you're so far away. I wonder where you are when I can't hear what you say."

* * *

"Are you ready to talk to me again?" Jeannette says coyly.

"Of course. Why do you ask?"

"I thought you might be bored with me. *He* gets bored with me—with most things. We were playing tennis once and when it was his serve, he shot three balls at once at me. When I asked him why he did that, he said he was bored."

"On the flip side, he might have been trying to be funny—clownish."

"I was winning. *He* threw my game off. It wasn't funny. *He* made me small. *He* always made me small."

"This is when the fuck would have come in handy. You know, the 'Fuck you!' Then you walk off, and *He* is so surprised, *He* laughs, implores you to return and starts to play seriously again, and it's a good afternoon."

"Well, Dr. Freud, I didn't say that. But I did walk off. We didn't talk for two days."

"You said *He* always *made* you small. Have things changed?"

"Well—obviously. Now that *He's* gone."

"Gone! When did *that* happen?"

"Last year. I must have told you."

"No," he says, deflated. "You didn't. You've been speaking as though he was right there in the house with you."

"It doesn't matter."

"How can you say that? We agreed I'd wait until you were free." Fred is still confused, as confused as the evening she broke up with him while they sat on a bench in Mapleton Park two months after he'd returned to the States. "You're a bundle of con-tradictions," Fred says more with sadness than anger. "Once you told me you married *Him* because he was lighthearted, more fun than me, that you took his ring because *He* gave you a way out: 'Try it on for size,' you said *He* said. 'Give it back whenever you want.' Then you tell me *He* wasn't fun at all. And now you say *He's* been gone for—I don't know how long—and you still cannot commit to me."

"People change. For God's sake, you of all people should know that." Her retort is almost heartless.

"They don't really change at all; they learn to deal: to cover, to squelch, to push through, redefine, manage, accept, cope. But they never change."

"Honestly, Fred, you're as depressing as ever."

"There must have been something good about *Him* for you to have stayed with *Him*. Something more than children and grand-children. And don't lie to me—again."

"Yes, there were good things besides caretaking and death, financial booms and busts. You build a life together—a marriage. How's that for positivity?"

"I expected more from you after all this time."

"Fuck you!"

"That's the most honest thing you've said in ages."

* * *

"How long has it been since we last spoke?" Jeannette asks.

"I don't know: months, years."

"Don't exaggerate."

"A long time."

"Where are you this morning, Freddie?"

"The waist. Mission eighteen. Second time I've ridden as a waist gunner. Our bombardier doesn't seem to care for the nose turret anymore—claims he's had too many close calls. The original left waist gunner rides the nose and the ball remains empty. I believe soon they'll be removing the ball turrets from all the ships because it's difficult to fly formation with them."

"Thank God! I hate to think of you alone in that capsule below the belly. Were you scared in there?"

"I'm scared everywhere. Damn! It's still very cold up here today—especially in the waist. The temperature has dropped to thirty-seven below zero. Chills are running through my body, vibrating me. My feet and hands are alarmingly cold; my heated shoes and gloves have burned out. I hit them continuously. I'm so afraid of frostbite; it usually results in amputation because of gangrene. Other than that, I think it will be what we call a milk run: flak is light, friendly fighter cover is staying with us all the way in and out. Bombed a factory at an airfield near St. Pol. We're flying ship number four fifty-two, the only ship in the squadron that has twenty-nine missions without having turned back because of mechanical failure."

"I thought your plane was the *Laurie Belle*."

"Lieutenant Meek, a pilot who flew across with us in our ship, shared the *Laurie Belle* with us when we weren't alerted for a mission. He took it over Berlin last week, but he never got back. The plane was under continuous attack and he was unable to bring it back to base, was forced to ditch in the Channel."

"All gone?"

"Some were believed to have bailed out over France. Lieutenant Meek's body was washed up on the English coast. Only the bombardier, another good buddy of mine, was thought to have been picked up by an air-sea rescue launch, but he was found floating unconscious in the water."

"When did you first realize it?"

"What?"

"The futility of war."

"My third mission. That's when I fully comprehended what was happening. We bombed Germany and actually got to see bombs bursting, knowing that people were being killed below. To see German fighters coming in at our formations and shooting down our bombers, to see men fighting against men, just didn't seem

right. Why should men want to kill each other, making war—life—
so miserable for everyone? It's not human. It's not right. I pray the
turmoil will end soon and that maybe there'll be peace among us
for generations to come. But here I still am."

"Here we all still are. Would you like to meet soon, Freddie?"

"I can't think about that now. I can't think about anything until
we land."

* * *

"I have obligations. I have children to help, grandchildren to care
for. My daughter is getting a divorce. I'm needed here." Jeannette
informs Fred with authority.

"*I* need you."

"But do you *want* me?"

"That's a silly question."

"No, it's not. They're not the same, you know. I used to think
you could learn to live without anybody. My father once told me
when I was a girl that if a man said he couldn't live without me, I
shouldn't want him."

"And now?"

"I'd like to be needed by a man. I'd like to be wanted."

* * *

"I'm free today! They are all in school or work or wherever. They're
all busy. I can take an early morning flight and be there for lunch."
She's almost giddy.

"I can't talk right now," Fred says, as though he didn't hear a
word she said. "We're close to the target and the flak is intense!"

"What's the target?"

"A German synthetic oil plant. Don't ask questions like that
now. Fuck! I just saw three of our B-24s go down! One was in a
nose spin plummeting down. Goddamn, the flak is so accurate, so
close! I just heard one about a foot away from me rip through the

fuselage. The bombs are away but the flak keeps coming. I'm frightened. We're going to lose seven planes today."

"You know that?"

"Of course I do."

"Call me when you land."

He doesn't reply. "Did you hear me?"

"Okay."

"Promise?"

"Promise."

"Which mission is it?"

"Number twenty-seven."

* * *

"You're crying!" Jeannette's eyes well up.

"Happens sometimes."

"Tell me about it."

"Guilt collides with gratitude. You never know who God will
choose to fly with. I guess He chose the first section of ships in our
group this morning because they missed their target. We were in
the second section, and when we went over the target, we caught a
terrific barrage of flak. One ship had its right rudder shot off and
had to make a crash landing at the base. Another plane got more
than eighty flak holes in it. Our tail gunner, Kirkpatrick, was killed
when a shell shot away the top of his turret. Krob went back to
give him a shot of morphine, but when he saw Kirkpatrick's brains
splattered all over the turret, he passed out. I went back to help
Krob, but I passed out, too."

* * *

"Everything's going wrong today: my heated rheostat won't work;
my left glove is on fire; my left boot is burning my heel, and now
I'll have a huge blister. To top it off, the interphone system has
been out most of the time! We're running into low fog and clouds

over the Channel and a terrific gale and are having a hell of a time trying to find our field. I don't know how much more of this I can take."

"You don't have to."

* * *

"Last Saturday we lost five of our buddies in the queerest circumstance. They were coming back from a raid on Hamm, Germany, and were over the Channel when Ju 88s opened up on the formation. A large force of German fighters had followed them back under cover of darkness and had attacked bomber bases simultaneously all along the coast. Air battles continued over the fields and there was so much confusion that ack-ack gunners were shooting down our own bombers!"

"Ack-ack?"

"You must have heard of the gunner gals in the Royal Artillery. Worked in pairs operating telescopes that located enemy aircraft, then sent the information to a predictor that calculated the exact time to shoot at and down a plane. They could do it all in a matter of seconds." He's perked up with excitement at the mention of them.

"They shot down planes?"

"No. Never. They were forbidden. The government said it was inappropriate, that life givers couldn't be life takers."

"How very British," Jeannette says, sarcasm laced with jealousy.

"The Ju 88s waited until one of our bombers turned on its lights to land and then came down on it, strafing with twenty-millimeter shells that hit the radio operator in the eyes and the first engineer squarely in the stomach. The ship was fucking burning up and they were forced to bail out. My buddy Grady was stunned and blinded; the crew put his 'chute on him and told him not to forget to pull the ripcord. He nodded that he understood, but he never did pull it. Another pal, Conway, wasn't wounded at all; later they found him drowned on the beach. The plane kept losing altitude fast, but the pilot and copilot stayed with the ship so the men could jump. The navigator, bombardier, tail gunner, and ball gunner bailed out safely. The nose gunner was seriously burned, especially in the face. I saw him today: he'll be permanently scarred. Still, he's thankful to have gotten away with his life."

* * *

"Jeannette, today will be remembered as one of the happiest days of my life."

"Happier than the day you met me at Orbach's during your summer job after high school graduation? Stock boy on his way to college meets switchboard operator?"

"It was. I have to admit. You need to understand the circumstances. It was, at that time, the happiest."

"Happier than the day you bought me the black galoshes with the gray cuffs at that shoe store on Fulton Avenue?"

He is silent. He can't remember.

"You do. You remember. You had just returned with the face of a twenty-year-old and eyes that had witnessed hell. You remember. It was Christmastime and we didn't know what to do with ourselves, as if everything we ever had to say to one another had already been said in letters. We walked like zombies, and as we neared the subway station, I suggested we take in the holiday displays in the store windows downtown. That's when you smiled for the first time since you'd returned—because you wanted to buy me something right then and there and not have to wait a few days to make me happy with the Christmas gift you'd already bought. It started to snow, and when we saw the shoe store, you smiled; you so wanted to make me happy. I pointed to the least expensive pair of boots. You smiled all evening, for the first time since you'd returned, carrying the box with my high heels, my feet warm and protected in the new boots."

"You've done it! You've made me happy by reminding me of that: as happy as I was that day. I wish you could see the grin on my face right now."

"I can," she says to assure him. "Smiles don't change."

"But I still haven't told you. Today I was awarded the Air Medal, and by Major Jimmy Stewart—the actor, no less! The gunner I just told you about got the Purple Heart."

"Metal, ribbon, and plastic. Hardly seems a consolation."

"But it is—at the time. You must understand that it is—desired, earned, and revered. I can hardly wait until I receive the Flying Cross after I've completed my missions."

"How do you know you'll get it?"

"Because I've been getting it for all these years."

"Was *She* pretty?"

"*She* was, in a pleasant way, if you know what I mean: nothing offensive or out of place—not even a hair—strong, but nothing remarkable."

"*She* probably didn't have a big nose like I do."

"No. Her nose fit perfectly with her face. As I said—unremarkable. Your nose has—"

"Don't say it. Please don't say it has character!"

He bursts into laughter. "Okay. No character. Just lots of individuality, strength, fire. And, by the way, it's not too big; it suits your face perfectly. When one looks at you, they're drawn in: first to the eyes—they sparkle—then the smile and the small sexy space between your front teeth, then the hair and nose. It's like an intriguing mosaic that holds your attention, keeps you mesmerized, figuring it out. Looking at *Her* was pleasant, like viewing a one-dimensional drawing or a chalky white plaster bust with indistinguishable features, pale blue eyes that lacked fire. I don't mean to be cruel. I've already said too much. But you asked me. That's how I saw *Her*. That's how *She* was."

"You've never shown me a picture of *Her*."

"Nor you of *Him*."

"Let's keep it that way."

"Yes, my love. Let's."

* * *

"I have a confession to make today, Jeannette, darling. Once, and only once, when I was away, I strayed."

"How far?" Jeannette asks.

"Quite far—the farthest. But only once, one day. Not *even* a day—a few hours. I shouldn't have said anything."

"Then why did you?" She teeters between anger and tears.

"Because we are mature now. Beyond mature. We are wise. And with wisdom comes honesty, and I want you to know everything."

"Why don't you just say you called today to torture me for breaking up with you? Are we even now?"

"It's hardly the same. It was a few hours, like I said. I was lonely."

"You must have been smitten with her. I know you. You must have been *very* smitten."

"Of sorts. She was an Ack-Ack Girl—one of those gunner gals."

"I knew there was something more about them! Where did you meet her?"

"At a pub. You must have met other servicemen home on furlough."

"Yes," she says coldly. "On the subway, at USO dances."

"And?"

"I talked with them some. I danced with them."

"You didn't kiss them?"

"If I did, I won't let myself remember. I hate this conversation."

"What else?"

"A few asked me to write to them."

"And did you?"

"I wrote one—to be kind—but my first letter came back saying he had been killed in action."

"Any others?" He persists.

"One."

"And?"

"I married *Him*. Satisfied?"

* * *

"I'm so glad you finally decided to come," he says to Jeannette one morning after so many mornings of silence.

"And you're not away at war. How fortunate! I've been afraid of the climate. I thought it would be colder here."

"I told you nothing was like being up in a bomber."

"You were right. Though I've never been in a bomber." She giggles. "And it's so much easier to breathe here than I'd imagined."

"That part—the getting here—is always the hardest."

"So, what do you think? How do I look?"

"The same, my love."

"Still a mosaic?"

"A spectacularly glittering one."

"All this traveling has worn me out: I'm afraid I'm a bit tired. You'll call me tomorrow morning after your mission? I want to wake up to the sound of your voice."

"Every morning. Get some rest. I can't wait to show you around after I land. Would you like me to sing to you now? Will it put you to sleep?"

"Oh, would you?"

"What do you want to hear?"

"You know the one. The one my mother used to sing all the time."

He begins to hum.

"Yes," she says groggily. "That's the one."

"I'll see you in my dreams," he croons. "Hold you in my dreams. Someone came and took you away …"

The Intruder

"You 'ave a lover?" the woman sitting in the armchair at the table next to me asked.

I didn't even look up. Whoever had said it couldn't have possibly been speaking to me, a stranger in a café in Downtown Crossing. Then she asked again.

"You 'ave a lover?"

I barely lifted my head to see who she and her silent companion were. She sat alone. The question had indeed been directed at me, who she continued to face head-on.

She was much older than me—maybe in her late fifties, early sixties—milky white skin with a raspy smoker's voice and heavy black eyeliner, intentionally smudged at the corners of her brown eyes, that was apparent even behind large red-framed glasses with rhinestone-studded gold temples: the kind of specs I would have thought way too outlandish for me, but that looked perfectly attractive sitting on the bridge of her slender, almost pointed, nose. It was all framed by chin-length, blunt-cut, straight jet-black hair parted down the center; glistening silver hoops dangling from her ears peeked through, catching the welcome rays of spring sunlight streaming through the window. I guessed at the accent: Middle Eastern? But her complexion was far too fair for most women from that part of the world, though there were always exceptions.

"Are you speaking to me?" I asked.

"Obviously."

"I'm married," I said, hoping to shut her up, but she only let out a haughty laugh that drew the attention of the barista behind the counter.

"You are not. No ring. Besides, in France, everyone 'as a lover."

"You mean the men," I said in a low voice, hoping she would follow my lead.

"I mean ze women too," she said as loudly as before.

"The last time I checked, this wasn't France," I said. I was becoming emboldened and intrigued to see where this was going, yet at the same time eager to shut her up.

"I bet you wear cotton panties too," she said. "American women, they are so practical."

Okay, that did it. I took one last sip of my cappuccino (which I'm sure she was critiquing as being a breakfast drink unsuited for late afternoon), collected my purse and my plastic Macy's bag, and walked out. I was halfway down the street when she fell in with my stride, her patent-leather high heels providing more clatter than my sensible flats.

"You sink I am crazy, some deranged person. Maybe I 'ave a pistol in my purse, or better yet a sharp letter opener. Isn't zat so? But I am not."

"I think you'd better walk away before I scream."

She breathed deeply, as though taking a long drag on a cigarette, and exhaled with a sigh. "I don't mean to frighten you or intrude. I merely noticed what an attractive woman you are and was hoping you were not denying yourself ze benefit and pleasure zat many of we French women of all ages enjoy. I understand zat eet is a cultural sing, but eet doesn't 'ave to be. Can I ask where you are going?"

At that point I didn't know where I was going. I had already passed the T station and had just kept walking with determination, hoping to shed her as one tries to do with a stray cat. But like a stray cat, she refused the hint. I stopped short—so short that she had to turn back a few feet to rejoin me.

"Would you like to sit in ze park and discuss zis?" she asked.

"No!"

"I sink you would, ozerwise you would not be still standing here beside me."

I wanted to give her a piece of my mind—say, Who the hell do you think you are? But she was right: I had passed the T station and not taken my leave of her. I headed for the entrance to the Common. In perfect synchrony—her bare arm brushing mine, her wafting spicy perfume like a leash around my neck—she followed. She was either coming on to me or pimping for some guy. On the other hand, she could have been a visiting professor—Boston was full of them—doing an anthropological or sex study: a modern-day Dr. Ruth or Masters and Johnson.

"What do you do?" I asked, both of us sitting down on the first bench we came to.

"What does eet matter? I don't care what *you* do. Everyone in America always wants to know how someone else earns a living. Zat is of no interest to me."

"Well, excuse me, but one does have to survive. And all this probing, this interrogation, might be associated with your job."

"You are trying to justify zat we can speak on the topic."

"No!"

"Yes."

"Okay, yes," I said.

"May I know your name?"

"Kathleen."

"Look, Kasleen. I can see zat you are an intelligent woman. How you use your intelligence is of no concern to me. I too have a career. But zat is not ze issue 'ere."

"Are you a reporter?"

"Oh, *mon dieu*, absolutely not! Nayvere! What is of relevance to me 'ere and now is 'ow you use your sexuality: Do you ignore it? Do you fulfill it? Do you deny it?"

I told her again that I was married.

"Zo you deny eet."

"I didn't say that."

"But yes, you did. And stop zis saying you are married. You are not."

"Why do you care about my sexuality—"

"Elise."

"Elise. I am nothing to you. You must have a motive."

"What ees in za bag?"

"None of your business."

"Ees intimate apparel, no?"

"Yes."

"Silky wiz lace? A song perhaps?"

I didn't answer.

"I knew eet! Eet ees cotton. Mebbe eet goes up to your waist," she said with disgust.

"It does not. It's bikini style—on sale."

"Well, sank goodness for zmall fayvors," she said with some sarcasm. "Why would any woman wear zose when you can luxuriate in somesing sensual zat will only enhance your erotic desires? *You* look to *dampen* zem."

I had to admit to myself that I had no answer for her. She was on the mark: I did feel sexier in risqué undergarments, but I chose to be practical—or, as she would say, unattractive and boring. But there was no one in the picture to see my intimate apparel nowadays. Hadn't been for quite a long time.

"You wear your underwear like a belt of chastity," she said.

"Oh, please!"

"Which you find more attractive: cotton briefs—or bikini ones—or low-cut satin zat reveals a fringe of pubic hair?"

I looked up sheepishly to see if the old man across from us had heard. He continued to systematically pinch off pieces of bread from a loaf in the white paper bag he held tightly in the crux of his free arm to feed a flock of pigeons. His preoccupation with the birds convinced me that he was hard of hearing.

"Everyone is more attracted to the latter."

"Most likely. I will admit, mebbe not everyone. But, yes, ze majority. Zo, why not you?"

"I have underwear like that!" I said.

"Hidden in ze back of your drawer. Zaved for a special occa-sion. Maybe someone else's wedding or an intimate encounter zat will not present itself because you deny your sexuality. Don't come near me, your body says. I am not desirable. Ze shop is closed for business."

I looked again at the old man who was now staring admiringly at Elise, although I was certain he hadn't made out a word of our conversation. He was of no significance: he was ancient. Then a cou-ple hardly out of their teens strolled along the path that separated us, their colorfully tattooed arms wound around each other's backs, their hands tucked deep into the other's low waistband, where they were overtly fishing. After they passed, the young man turned his head—shaved along the temples, black curls sprouting from the crown like water from a fountain—to catch a second glimpse, not of me, the woman closer to his age, but of Elise. Elise the interest-ing one. Elise who signaled availability, generated desire or, at the very least, curiosity.

"Ah, *l'amour* as fresh as ze new green of spring," she said, with a satisfaction that probably derived more from the boy's fleeting attention than the couple's obviously raging hormones. "When was your last time, Kasleen?"

"For what?"

"Oh, please! Do not be coy. Eet ees most unbecoming."

"Awhile. Let's leave it at that."

She pursed her lips and shook her head at the pity of it all.

"And ze big breakup. Ze one zat has made you sink zat because he rejected you, no one else wants you."

"That's not what I think."

"Time, eet passes quickly, Kasleen. Today you are maybe sirty? Sirty-five?" Her pronunciation gave that age a dreaded and dirty connotation. "Before you know, you will be fifty. And alone. I am not speaking about marriage necessarily. Not even children. Ze loneli-ness zat comes from wasted pleasure.'Ave you ever been to an orgy?" she asked, as though asking if I'd ever tasted strawberry ice cream.

"No!"

She laughed heartily.

"Of course you 'ave not. Eet ees all right, Kasleen. Really." She patted me on the hand and laughed again.

Her cell phone sounded, and she fished it out of her large soft leather purse.

"*Oui, oui, bien sûr, mon cher. A bientôt.* I am on my way." She sang in a sultry tone I resented, envious of the caller who was taking her away from me. I had simply been a way for her to kill time. "Well, it has been lovely, Kasleen. I am zo glad to 'ave met you."

With that, she leaned over and gave me a peck on both cheeks, got up, and walked briskly out of the park, hailing the first taxi that was headed her way. Of course, its roof light signaled that it was, like her, available.

Without giving it a second thought, I carried my purchases back to Macy's and exchanged them for several pairs of full-price satin and lace panties, a thong, and a low-cut, see-though, black mesh bra. After paying, I grabbed another item off a rack and took it into the dressing room on the pretense of trying it on. Protected by a full-length mirror with large wings on either side, a locked louvered door, and two wire racks—one for Keepers and the other for Rejects—I removed my underwear and put on the silky low-cut panties I had just bought. The sight of my dark pubic hair peeking out from the lace-trimmed top of the panties sent my hand to my crotch: Not now, not here, I told myself, envisioning some man sitting in a room littered with dirty coffee cups and greasy fast-food containers, its walls lined with security cameras showing views of so-called private places like these. I quickly took off my white underwire bra and put on my new one, whose spaghetti straps threatened to snap under the weight of my ample breasts, those smooth, latte-colored mounds with nipples now excited and erect. I smiled at the image before me. Elise's image smiled approvingly in the wings.

* * *

It had grown even muggier when I stepped outside, the Macy's bag with my old clothing dangling from one arm, my raincoat casually draped over the other. I was still wearing a sweater, but it was form-fitting and pale-colored, generously displaying the outline of my new bra and all that it attempted to contain. While my panties were hidden beneath my jeans, they lent to my swagger. I had assumed the gait my grandmother used to tell me to walk with, the swaying hips Sophia Loren had—advice I had rejected as being old-fashioned and sexist.

The rush-hour subway car I boarded was filled to capacity. Lucky to get a seat, I watched men and women being jostled as they tried to stay erect by hanging on to poles or straps. I remembered a film in which every morning two strangers on their way to work boarded the same New York City car. The man entered first and joined a group clustered around the nearest pole. The woman stepped onto the car at the next stop and smoothly inserted herself into the crowd attached to the same pole, her back to the man, the two of them sandwiched together. As the train rolled, rhythmically jerking along its track, it became obvious that both were deriving sexual pleasure. They never spoke, and without so much as a glance, got off at different stops.

Given their intense attraction to each other, the man fell in love with the woman and assumed she had with him. He broke off his engagement to his fiancée and one morning asked his fellow commuter for a date. To his shock, the woman, without uttering a word, was clearly outraged at the notion, got off at the next stop, and never appeared on the same train again. A woman who seeks the thrill of physical pleasure in public with a stranger seemed unfathomable to me—absurd. And yet there I was, eyeing each passenger, wondering if anyone was engaging in such clandestine consensual activity; looking to see if there might be a candidate with whom I could envision myself engaging in such an ostensibly innocent but pleasurable scenario.

Call what followed next kismet, but a man about my age boarded the car and took a seat that had just been vacated. As usual, I tried to ignore him, but it was impossible to not take in his attire, his haircut, his velvety skin tone. Too casually dressed in a pinchecked shirt and jeans, with no tie or jacket, to be a lawyer. No scrubs signaling an intern or resident. Perhaps a banker, salesman, baker, candlestick maker? Too upscale even for a graduate student. There you go again. "What do you care what he does?" Elise whispered in my ear.

We riders of the T are adept at observing minute details of one another while pretending not to pay the slightest attention, feigning to study the Massachusetts Bay Transportation Authority map we know by heart or ads that hold little interest, or appearing to be dozing behind heavy eyelids that only give the impression of being shut. And when we do stare, it is with a blank expression that indicates *I'm not really seeing you; I just have to land these peepers somewhere.* But all the while we're seeing every sweaty brow, every red nose being blown into a crumpled tissue, every stubby finger, every artistically manicured or dirty chewed-up nail checking cell phone messages. And all the while we're conjecturing, forming hypotheses for individuals we know absolutely nothing about.

Then I did the extraordinary: I faced him head-on and, as we exchanged smiles, took him in, from his glistening black hair, midnight eyes, and fine physique down to his liberated hands, free of any briefcase, purchase, umbrella, or wedding ring.

"This is my stop." I broke the silence, daring to shrug and signal regret as the rumbling train that had climbed out of darkness and up to street level—too soon—came to its Brookline stop.

"Can I call you?" he asked as I stood up.

"Yes."

"Do you have a card or something?" I shook my head. X-ray technicians don't usually carry cards. Since there was no time for him to take down my information, he hastily pulled a wallet out of his back pocket and took out a card of his own.

"Call me?" he politely asked rather than instructed—a definite plus.

I nodded, taking the card and heading for the open doors as I ran to my apartment building and up to the third floor. Happy. Happy. Happy.

* * *

We spoke that evening, although I have no recollection of his name or his occupation. That's of little consequence to my story, for he was certainly earnest and intriguing enough for me to follow through with our rendezvous. It's the preparation—the showering, the careful shaving of legs and underarms and the tweezing of eyebrows to catch every stray hair, the painstaking application of makeup, the donning of dress and jewelry, all of it executed under impossible deadline to arrive promptly at the agreed-upon destination—that stands out. The excitement that stirred inside me. The yearning to be drawn close to him, to feel his chest against mine, to kiss him long and passionately.

I don't remember how I arrived at our meeting place. On foot? By car? Sitting on the T or in the back seat of an Uber? What lingers in my mind is the elation that overcame me upon seeing the eager expression of the man from the train, the sensation of longing that propelled me toward him before an unrecognizable disturbance occurred: a shattering of the world around me, and of the moment in time.

Confusion, disappointment, gratitude for the place where I'd landed. Eyes still shut, I reached out with my sleep-weakened hand for reassurance of the familiar torso that had on countless nights covered my frame more perfectly than my own stubborn flesh was capable of. I gave thanks for having averted the pain of the heartbreak that most assuredly would have resulted had my impossible romance ever played out in real time. I gave thanks for a love dragged through life's muddy trenches that had come out whole, yet still feeling the need to apologize for my spiritual infidelity, for the fierce carnal grasp the stranger had had on me.

I strained in frustration to hang on to the romance, to the sight of the smiling face that was now detached from its body and receding from me, drifting farther and farther into space until, like a lost astronaut, it sailed out of sight. And desire received permission to mourn for a few moments without interruption. Not for the stranger, but for youth.

Amnesia

She flew out to San Francisco on September 19, the Saturday morning of what was supposed to have been her rehearsal dinner but which had become a disconcerting day to fly in any event, not to mention the pandemic that was currently gripping the nation. Six days in a cushy hotel room, the first stage of quarantine—a honeymoon for one, of sorts, with daily COVID-19 tests, room service, all the desserts she desired, and brief masked walks around the building.

She hadn't intended to do a second summer tour of duty at the Brighton research station in Antarctica. Her first had been three years earlier, while Jack, her boyfriend, was studying for the bar exam and hardly noticed her absence. This time around she was supposed to have been on her honeymoon, basking on the sunny shores of Aruba. Of course, the pandemic would have nixed that and the wedding date all by itself, would have postponed everything for at least a year, until a vaccination had been discovered, approved, and administered to the one hundred and ninety guests who were to have packed the Boston Park Plaza Hotel ballroom. But she and Jack had already waited ten years since they had met at her college friend's wedding—he the escort of an alum she'd always found insufferable. What would another year have meant to them?

"The longer you wait, the more failings you discover about a person," her father kept telling her. "That doesn't mean you shouldn't marry them," he added. "Everyone dislikes certain aspects about their mate that can be managed. It doesn't mean you won't live a happy life—for the most part. But if you discover the flaws that are sure to come too soon, you'll never tie the knot." He recited various European adages: *Before you get married, take a good look at what you're doing*, the Spanish would warn. *After the confetti come the defects*, the Italians insisted. Still, she waited, confident about her decision to marry and laughing at what she considered to be absurd advice.

She waited until they had enough money for a sizable down payment on a duplex condo in the heart of downtown Boston. Until Jack was well established in a large law firm that put no caps on its swelling number of partners. Until Nicole had decided what she was best suited to do in life and obtained a master's degree in public health, then yet another in human resources. Until one day, as Jack hurriedly set out for a tennis date, he tripped on the third step on the staircase of their new home and tumbled the rest of the way, hitting his head on several of the uncarpeted wooden treads and giving it a final whack on the tile floor of the foyer where he landed.

Ten days in the hospital, test after test, assurances that the confusion, the blurred vision, the balance issues, and memory problems almost always faded following a loss of consciousness after this type of brain injury. Doctors described a woman whose crazed husband had hit her several times in the head with a hedge trimmer while she lay sleeping; the woman was able to describe the event in gory detail the moment she came to. But while most of Jack's symptoms did indeed disappear, so did his long-term memory: he couldn't recognize his parents and brothers, let alone Nicole, in the weeks after he woke from his coma.

A memory specialist promised hope. He taught Jack different ways to increase what memory he had: keep driver's license, cell phone, and keys all in one place—at home. Create a password log of sorts, identifying not just things but people and their relationship and importance to him.

In time he reacquainted himself with his life and those who had occupied it alongside him. The mechanics of corporate law returned, and what didn't come back he was able to pick up handily. While it wasn't certain that he recalled individuals—friends, coworkers, and family—the determined young man relaxed with them and became comfortable once again coordinating dinners and outings he had initially been hesitant to arrange.

A blurry memory of Nicole also returned: she was the fiancée, the woman with whom he had been about to commit to spend the rest of his life and grow a family. She didn't mind the prompting he needed to recall her age, her allergies, how she took her coffee, or what sexual position she fancied most. He was trying—doing the best he could do—until he couldn't do it anymore. He couldn't love her. He didn't even like her.

"I told you not to wait," her father said.

"Better you did," her mother said, "before children were involved—and more real estate."

* * *

"What does an HR person do in Antarctica?" the guy sitting two seats away from her at the airport had asked after she told him what she did in the "real world," as he called it.

"Pretty much the same thing one does back home. Personal issues compounded tenfold. You know, the roommate drama and bad behavior found in any college dormitory or bar. So, I guess you can say I'm an HR-RA there." She flashed a closed-mouth grin that implied *How's that for an answer?* But it appeared behind her mask, so he didn't see it.

"Cool."

How did flakes like him get selected to join the cohort? she wondered. *Must be one of the Wasties, the small team that packaged up everything from Food and Recycling to Hazardous and Sani Waste in shipping containers. Even that task had to be meticulously handled so that waste was collected, segregated, and shipped according to all laws and regulations. Did this guy have any idea about the operations it took to support science at the bottom of the world, or was he utterly preoccupied with his inability to get laid for the next three weeks of quarantining?* she asked herself, fully acknowledging that her tolerance of male behavior was at an all-time low. After all, she'd taken on this assignment to help erase memories of having been dumped by her longtime love.

The fellow seemed to have trouble following rules from the get-go on this first leg of their journey. She took her allowed morning constitutional and circled the Bay Area hotel in which she and two hundred others from the program were quarantining. It was no coincidence that the same individuals picked the same time of day to walk. She had learned in her studies in human resources that it took just one time—one time—for humans to create a pattern: heading for the same seat on the school bus every day; sitting at the same table in the cafeteria, the same chair at family holiday dinners; vying for the same parking space in the company lot. It became their seat, their space, their chair, as they took possession of things that in no way belonged to them. And so it went at the hotel. There was no need to assign recreational time slots: on the first day everyone claimed their own, signed in and out at a particular hour, and maintained the required six-foot spacing—everyone, that is, but this guy. Each time she lapped the building, he closed in on her like a racehorse accelerating his gait, attempting to pin her to the rail as she tried to move closer to the building and away from him.

"Do you *mind?*" she said one day, not attempting to conceal her annoyance.

"I kind of do," he said. "The social distancing, that is. And you make it that much harder."

If that was supposed to have been a compliment, she didn't buy it. The next day she chose to walk at a different time. However, he had clearly checked the sign-out sheet, and for the remainder of their days there, he walked when she did, keeping step with her and making her grateful for the requirement that they spend the rest of their time alone in their rooms.

* * *

They had another two-week government-managed isolation stay in Christchurch before they could head to the ice, precautions taken by all member countries of the Antarctic Treaty committed to keeping Antarctica COVID-free. Though some routine projects had been canceled because of the pandemic, it was imperative for the Brighton station to remain operational. This meant making safety the year's top priority.

She hadn't tried a periodic email update her last time in Antarctica because she hadn't felt the need to communicate; thoughts of Jack and their future together dispelled any moments of loneliness. But this time around, she had no sooner landed in Christchurch than she began to feel the emptiness. She tried to entice family and friends to communicate via snail mail by promising to send them artful postcards postmarked from Antarctica, meanwhile assuring those who voiced disinterest in her email updates that she would delete them from her address group.

In Christchurch, their outdoor time was unlimited. Wearing masks and social distancing, they were free to roam what they called the prison yard—a small gravel pen of sorts—where they resembled madmen walking around in tiny circles to exercise, all the while being photographed by curious Kiwis and guarded by New Zealand security to ensure that nobody made a run for it. After a few days, black fabric was draped over the construction fence exterior so the Kiwis couldn't peer in at the wild American animals who could not look out.

"This country gives new meaning to the Ugly American," he, who continued to follow her recreational schedule, said as she tried to reverse direction. "I mean, like they're so fucking clean here. Like they couldn't get the China virus if they fell into a petri dish."

"For the record, it's COVID, and I hope that's the last time I hear you refer to it that way."

"My mom had it. Almost didn't make it. All this quarantining, people dying, losing their jobs and businesses didn't have to happen."

"But it did. It *is* happening. Just hope we don't get stuck here for another three weeks like the group who came earlier did."

"No shit! Why?"

"Horrible weather—flying and landing conditions. Look—what's your name?"

"Sean. It's on my name tag. Underneath all the outerwear. Sean Rollins Theberge the Third. Your turn. And by the way, stink bugs came from there too—in boxes of shipped goods."

She had resisted telling him her name. How crazy was that? Anyone could look her up. Everyone was going to know who she was once they got settled at Brighton. Still, she felt a desire to maintain distance between them. "Nicole," she said. "You must admit they're doing a damn good job of keeping this country COVID-free. I mean, the way they handle things swiftly and without all the self-defeating red tape our government goes through. Look how the prime minister responded to that mass shooting in the mosque. A gun law was put into place in one day!"

He stopped in his tracks and gave her a cold stare. "Guns don't kill. People do." Then he wheeled and headed back into the hotel.

Well now, she had finally learned how to deter him: say anything that made him think she was anti-American. She tried to chuckle, but some phlegm caught in her throat and she nearly gagged as she envisioned what the next four months with Sean Rollins Theberge could do to her and the other three hundred forty-eight Americans among whom she was charged with keeping peace.

* * *

She entered the roomy US Air Force C-17 Globemaster on a Tuesday morning in early October, accepting the bag lunch she was handed and proceeding to a jump seat, making sure to secure one already occupied on both sides. She put on headphones and prepared to entertain herself for the five-hour flight to McMurdo as though she were destined for Paradise Island.

Sean was among the last to board. When he finally settled into one of the few vacant seats remaining, his eyes found hers and he smiled with what appeared to be relief. She smiled back and shut her eyes, returning her attention to the music coming from her headphones and trying to erase the image of his foot nervously tapping the floor, his flushed face relaxing at the sight of her. She felt pity for him that morning and a different kind of burden. She had seen false bravado before in her line of work. She had seen how it made men behave badly, and she had had to confront it and impose consequences. Once at Brighton they'd be free of the world's ongoing nightmare; they'd also be stranded together, each preoccupied about those back home. She would have to show extra strength, extra patience. She could do this. She nodded along to the music and then fell asleep. She woke up feeling peaceful.

The collective tranquility aboard the Globemaster gave way to nervous energy when the pilot's "Welcome to Antarctica, where the temperature is a pleasant, dry five degrees Fahrenheit" reminded his passengers of the reality of the place where they would be confined for the next four months. She already knew that the weather wasn't that bad if you dressed properly. It was the winds limiting visibility to less than a hundred feet that made the climate brutal, forcing people into the nearest shelter until the storm passed.

Unlike her thrilling experience after landing on her last tour of duty, she felt like a child abandoned by her mother on the first day of preschool when, emptied of its passengers, the plane quickly departed before more damage would be done to the ice runway. She had taken the time during the flight to reevaluate how she was going to deal with Sean and anyone else like him. She was aware of the need for impartiality and not letting personal issues cloud her vision. Her job was to support and sustain the ongoing year-round scientific endeavor and ensure that the station remained operational against all odds.

* * *

Due to the reduction in staff that COVID regulations caused, each team member was assigned their own dorm room. This was a relief to Nicole, who on her last tour had had to deal with a woman who refused to talk to her—not one word. The woman was using her residential time at Brighton as a form of "verbal cleansing," and while she spoke when it was demanded of her, her time in the room was restricted to infrequent notes or hand signals, or no communication at all. "How's this working out for you?" Nicole asked one night as her roommate, seated in the lotus position on her bed, buried her face in the latest book she had borrowed from the station's library. The woman looked up with evident annoyance. *What don't you get about this?* her expression said. That was the last time Nicole spoke to her, except for when she sang. After all, she wasn't determined to be silent, and singing was better than talking to herself.

* * *

"I'm starting to worry that we'll run out of beer," Sean said during an appointment he'd made to see her in her official workspace. "I mean, what if the planes can't land or the ships that carry it get stuck somewhere. You know, like in the Suez Canal. So, I'm think-ing that we should brew our own. Or maybe hire a full-time brewer: I hear there's one on an Australian base."

Nicole couldn't completely muffle the outburst of laughter she tried to disguise as a cough and, burying her mouth in the crook of her arm, she turned away from him. Staring into his earnest and desperate face would have been unbearable.

"They do brew at a New Zealand base a mile and a half away," she said, regaining her composure. "Maybe you can take a dogsled there one day if we run out. As for Brighton—no dice. No living non-native species on-continent." She managed a sympathetic grin.

"Then what are we doing here?" he asked, causing them both to laugh. "How about a beer later tonight, Nicole?"

"I want to try and post some pics before everyone gets online or I'll be up until two a.m. waiting for the net to lighten up. Having four hundred and fifty people sharing the bandwidth capacity of a 4G smartphone is brutal."

"Well, if you have trouble early on, come down to the bar. We can kill time there." He smiled. He had straight white teeth she wondered if he whitened. She had an aversion to stained enamel.

As much as she hated to admit it, there was something more appealing about Sean than his teeth. She'd always been a sucker for blue eyes. Jack has blue eyes. Her kindergarten boyfriend had blue eyes. And while she wasn't into the faux-innocent boyish look of surfer blonds, she liked Sean's sandy hair shaved close at the temples with platinum curls that resembled swirls of frosting at the crown. Probably has a wife and kid—or two—back home, but bare ring fingers on a gig like this said don't ask, don't tell. Forget the caveats about the golden rules of dating, she told herself, because there would be no relationship for her on this tour.

She wrote home about the Weddell seals all over the sea ice and the emperor penguins that should be starting to arrive, though they were mostly solitary in this area, and the ones she sighted were usually off in the distance molting or, like her, separated from their mates—or lost. She told everyone that skuas had appeared: scavenger birds that literally swoop down and take the food right out of your hand. It's a violation of the Antarctic Conservation Act to interact with or bother wildlife, the rule being: stay well away from animals. If they're reacting to you, you're too close. Her fire chief said the same rule could apply to men's behavior toward women in the bars.

* * *

Sean seemed to be settling in just fine after the first week, enjoying the relief of his Level Green status: no quarantine, no mask.

"I hiked six miles today on that trail system over volcanic rock!" he said, pulling out the chair beside her that he had claimed as his place at dinner.

"You can rent cross-country skis or fat-tire bikes for the trails, you know," said the woman sitting across from them and whose taco costume he took in with narrowed eyes.

"Cool. Biking on an ice sheet would be a first! Maybe we can do that someday." He was quick to include his fellow diners, which put Nicole at ease. He said he was headed for the fitness room after dinner to lift weights. "See you guys at the bar tonight?" he said.

"You shoot hoops?" Corey, a fellow supervisor asked. "How about a little one-on-one?"

"Yeah. Sure. But I might hit the climbing wall first. You game?" he asked Nicole.

"Think I'll grab a yoga class."

A man walked by in a unicorn onesie.

"Is Halloween early this year or something?" Sean remarked, scratching his head.

"Antarcticans love their—our—costumes," the woman in the taco suit said, laughing. "You can rent them from the gear-issue room. Makes life interesting."

"Whatever floats your boat." Sean raised his eyebrows and shrugged. "Catch you guys later." He picked up his tray of cleaned plates and took off.

"The guy's got a nonstop motor on him," Corey said. The woman in the taco suit nodded.

"Yeah—energetic," Nicole said.

He was, to Nicole's relief, adapting. With the quarantine restrictions lifted, he might as well have been a reluctant camper who had discovered the joys of being away from home. Nicole turned her attentions to the standard employee issues: benefit/payroll questions, conflicts between coworkers, dissatisfaction with supervisors, lots of training, and the bad behavior that almost always resulted from booze overconsumption. After three weeks she had restricted the alcohol privileges of over a dozen, sent several back to the States for medical reasons or refusing to take a flu shot, and fired two employees following separate investigations of harassment. She also deleted three emails she'd begun writing Jack, having convinced herself that his former memory must have surely returned by now—along with his love.

Yet despite their isolation, the COVID craziness remained alive and well at Brighton. Each time a flight came in with even one person who had endured the managed isolation and multiple COVID tests, the station went into what was called Level Yellow. That meant that for a seven-day stretch after the plane touched down, they had to adhere to social distancing requirements and wear masks in all public spaces; seating limitations were enforced at mealtimes; bars closed; social events were prohibited. There were even restrictions on how many people could be in a bathroom at one time. Level Yellow was extremely challenging for morale.

For the first time in the station's history, the principal goal had gone from that of supporting science to keeping Antarctica COVID-free, and Level Yellow was their last defense against the virus. For a multitude of reasons, they were enduring much more Yellow that season than had been anticipated. And, in turn, there was much more difficulty surviving a tour of duty. While the ultimate staffing goal was retention, since it took a lot of time, effort, and money to bring someone down here, for some people like Sean, it didn't always work out.

Sean grew increasingly agitated during a Level Yellow, storming off at mealtimes when he found his seat beside Nicole taken. Corey told her he had seen Sean trying to get a beer from the bar when drinking was off-limits. She said she'd take care of it, but not the way Corey had envisioned. She had admonished Sean but gone soft, giving him the benefit of the doubt, writing up a warning and tucking away a copy in her desk drawer. She had been right about him: he was a Wastie, and good at his job. That and his looks—and his attention—drew her to him. She had even begun to dream about him, about making love with him. He wouldn't refuse the opportunity, she knew, if given the chance. But it was against her principles for a woman in her position. If it went awry, they could both be discharged, and they already had enough problems with waste disposal without losing a vital member of that crew. This had been the first summer with no visit from a ship that brought food, beverages, mail, people, equipment, replacement parts, tools, machinery—you name it—to sustain the stations throughout the austral winter, when no flights arrived. The ice pier that accommodated ships had not been constructed in time due to major storms in spring followed by high temps in summer. Aside from bringing incoming cargo, the vessel was important for removing all of Brighton's waste. Waste disposal was so important; everything had to leave the continent. Trash sorting was a big deal.

There were trash centers in every dorm and work center. When you disposed of something, you placed it in a bin labeled Landfill, Food Waste, Hazardous Waste, Recycling, Sani Waste, or Skua— better known as the Goodwill or reusable bin. The small team of Wasties to which Sean belonged packed everything in shipping containers while ensuring that the waste was collected, segregated, and shipped by the book. Waste was allowed to remain on the continent up to two years: that meant that roughly 2.5 million pounds of solid waste and 500,000 pounds of hazardous waste, which included those from their stay during 2021, would not be placed on a vessel until 2022. Losing Sean at this time would indeed be a waste of manpower.

* * *

The only good thing about a Level Yellow was the celebration when it was lifted. The countdown clock made its appearance in the rec room, and it was New Year's Eve all over again as Brighton shifted to a no-restrictions Level Green. Each celebration seemed an attempt to outdo the last, as the prohibitions had only exacerbated the frustrations of disease, hardship, and the political climate back home. Two and a half months in and they were already on their third Level Green bash—costumes aplenty—when the masks flew off, the hugging and high-fiving abounded, and the alcohol was broken out. The most recent celebration included a drag show with both gay and straight participants, but it was several real divas who brought the house down.

"I hate this shit," Sean, dressed as a shirtless gladiator, was heard to have mumbled.

"You'd better tone that down, buddy," Corey said, having long ago lost any tolerance for Sean's attitude after he'd been asked to resolve the heated argument that evolved between Sean and several other plastered partyers.

"Fuck it! What happened to freedom of speech? Or does it only apply to queers?" Sean said.

Corey went to grab Sean by the arm, intending to lead him away, when a punch intended for Sean landed squarely on his jaw.

"Now look what you assholes did!" Sean cried, assuming the role of protector.

It was several women, including Nicole, who charged to the scene and broke up the scuffle.

In a normal summer, he and the others involved would have been gone in two or three days. But with the limited flights that year and the need to take the additional measure of alerting the New Zealand government about an incoming flight, a sober and contrite Sean was permitted to continue the work at which he was so competent until his departure could be scheduled. Tail wagging between his legs, he came seeking absolution from Nicole.

"I don't know what came over me," he said, shaking his head and nearly succumbing to tears. "I don't really feel that way. I don't! I mouth off sometimes, especially when I drink, but I don't really mean it. I hate it afterward."

She regarded him dubiously.

"It's the cold. The isolation. It's—you."

"Me?"

"Yeah. You know. I like you, Nicole. I respect you. Have from the start. You unnerve me, frighten me—in a good way."

"This doesn't change anything, you know. Rules are rules."

She wanted to say she liked him too. The Sean, that is, without the prejudiced outbursts and insults. But she stood firm, silent about her own romantic desires and her intention to try to plead his case. Given this season's unusual conditions at the base, he might—just might—have a second chance. She believed him to be earnest. She had always prided herself on being a good judge of character; that's why she'd been drawn to the field of human resources.

* * *

It had been a super-cold week with temps averaging minus five Fahrenheit to minus one, with a minus thirty windchill. On sunny days Nicole tended to forget where she lived and neglected to put on a hat or gloves. She only needed to be outside for a minute before her nose hairs and digits began to freeze. It was on one such day, as she was walking back to her dorm from a meeting with other supervisors, when her extremities pointed out her misjudgment regarding her apparel. That's when she encountered Sean on his last day at Brighton. All attempts to plead his case had failed. He was carrying a massive battery belonging to a personnel carrier vehicle to its final resting place.

"Couldn't you charge it?" Nicole asked.

"Too much corrosion. Its time has come. What about my dismissal? Couldn't you fix that? You've got a lot of clout with everyone. It won't happen again. You know that."

"Too much corrosion," she said, and he nodded, disappointed.

"Want my hat and gloves?" He stopped and was about to put down the battery.

"No. But thanks. It's not much longer."

"By the way, what's the W stand for?" he asked.

"The W?"

"On your nametag, Nicole W. Hayes. I've been wondering for months. Let me guess. I'm good at names. Wendy."

"Nope."

"Wait, don't tell me! Winona, like the actress."

She laughed. "Wong."

"Wrong again? Let me try one more time."

"No. I said Wong. My mother's maiden name."

Was he looking at her now—at the slight fold of her upper eyelids, the only physical trait she had inherited from her mother and one too subtle to generate assumptions about her heritage, even in the twenty-four-hour daylight of an Antarctic summer? She couldn't tell. Freezing muscles contracted, naked hands tucked into her pockets, eyes focused on her warm destination in the distance, she might as well have been in the blinding dark of an Antarctic winter. She would not have seen his gaze, the stiffening of the jaw, the clenching of teeth, or the tightening of his sinewy arms around the battery. But she had begun to imagine things, as she often did in the surreal world of Brighton: she—not Jack—tumbling down the stairs and Jack coming to her rescue; she—not he—losing memory, which might have been a welcome gift in the aftermath of the pain she had suffered. For the first time in her stay, Nicole felt a terrifying aloneness and a fear that she could never again be certain of anything. There would be no time to detect the direction of Sean's swift movements if he made any. What if, without warning, she felt the bludgeoning, like the woman who'd been hit with the hedge cutter by her husband, and in this case the repeated impact of the hard metal of the battery against her skull, the implacable depth of hatred toward her that he might be harboring? He had cleverly clouded her discernment before. What if she had misjudged him completely, as she had Jack and their relationship?

What if?

You Can't Get There from Here

Thomas couldn't help himself: he'd been a breech birth—bottom up and out first. From that moment on he backed his way into every situation. He never pulled into a parking place like most drivers did; it was the rear end he guided in, claiming that this would make it easier to get out. "What's the difference if you back out or back in?" Colette would ask. But to Thomas there was a distinct difference; his mind couldn't see it any other way. In fact, he couldn't see most things any other way.

He'd had a girlfriend when he first met Colette. He always had another woman tucked away somewhere, either back home or at a different college or, later in life, in his apartment as his wife. He was what women labeled cute, with twinkling green Scottish eyes, a good athlete, and a hard drinker but not a self-destructive one. For a while, when he was working his way up the marketing corporate ladder, he'd had as many as three women in play at one time, their names all beginning with the letter *S*: Sandra, Sally, Sofia—a fact he found amusing. That was after his first and only wife had left him because he was running after Colette every chance he got.

"Leave your girlfriend," Colette had said when they were still in college. "Break your engagement and I'll date you," she said after they'd graduated. "Leave your wife, and we'll give it a go," she said when, as a married man, he showed up at her apartment door with his puppy-dog eyes and eager lips. But he didn't. Sometimes, when she was lonely, Colette gave in to his fawning: he was a charmer, a good kisser, a decent lover. What he wasn't was a man who could commit to the one woman he couldn't seem to live without, crazy as it seemed.

He had grown up surrounded by females: a mother acquiescent to his controlling father, three aunts, and five older sisters. When his father, the commander-in-chief, passed at a relatively early age, the role fell naturally to Thomas. He took it on, not out of ego or a need for power, but rather out of love—and obligation, and the determination to protect what his father called the fairer (but meant the weaker) sex. Yet most women Thomas met weren't weak at all; in fact, most were strong, and there lay the rub.

* * *

Once, before either of them had married, and he was studying at Wharton and she was teaching in an inner-city Philly school, he made a surprise visit to her fifth-grade class.

"You were amazing!" he said afterward. "Especially the way you handled the boy who peed his pants."

"He has a bladder dysfunction. Sometimes he forgets his special underpants."

"The kids didn't make fun of him."

"No. They've been taught to understand."

"You taught them."

She shrugged. "My job."

He had beamed with admiration: this was a woman who could understand him. Who did understand him far better than he understood himself. Yet he was, at the time, engaged to be married to that other woman—a demanding woman, but not a needy one. Someone he admired for her intelligence and, at the same time, feared. Someone he was not attracted to as much as he was to Colette. Someone who wouldn't cling to him the way his mother and sisters and aunts did. Someone he held at arm's length. Someone who eventually got fed up with him and left. If he had ever committed to Colette, he would never have been able to keep that distance between them. But this he wouldn't understand for a very long time.

He and Colette went on vacation after that visit to her school, although they did not go alone. They had never gone anywhere special alone except to bed. She wanted to go camping in Maine—to Acadia National Park—but his classmate's girlfriend had chosen the Jersey Shore. He couldn't disappoint his friend's girlfriend, he told Colette. After all, he and Colette were not boyfriend and girlfriend; they were just good friends. Thomas's real girlfriend—his fiancée—was on a volunteer medical mission in Honduras. And so they went to the beach, where they ate at restaurants the other woman, a proclaimed foodie, chose, and where they took the smallest bedroom, one with no windows, in the cottage that Colette was forced to clean each morning because the woman was a neat freak, and where Colette was expected to come up with culinary feasts, meals that never met the woman's standards. That was the last time he and Colette traveled together. It was the last time they did anything together. The following year she married another man.

What, he wondered from time to time, was this impulse he had to satisfy other women and not Colette? Why hadn't he ever been able to clear the way just for her? She had asked him this one time when they had met for lunch while she was in Philadelphia at a teachers' conference. He had looked down into his beer, said, "I was stupid," and gone on to admit, for the first and last time, that he had made a mistake.

He had called her, very excited, after he graduated from Wharton—MBA in hand and about to head to New York to a new job—to tell her he had been offered a better position in Philly and wouldn't be moving after all. Was she supposed to have been elated? He was married now. And if they were such good friends, why hadn't he invited her to his wedding? Because he and his wife had agreed there would be no former boyfriends or girlfriends, he told her—but according to Colette, his "girlfriend" was something she had never been.

It wasn't until Thomas began dating the three *S*'s that he felt free to risk losing all of them because the woman he desired had gotten married and was no longer available; that is to say, there was no longer a woman he needed to shield himself from Colette. He had never been able to choose among the three *S*'s anyway, convinced that all three were in his pocket until all three abandoned him. All five, if one counted Colette and his ex-wife. But he was never truly alone because there were those sisters who had been raised to be dependent and who continued to rely on him, especially as he grew more and more financially successful thanks to the increased competition created by the Internet and globalization. And in his mind there was always Colette out there somewhere. He would wait until she was free one way or another, and then he would have her—the love of his life, the rationale for all his failures with women. There wasn't anyone comparable. It had to be Colette.

* * *

There were long lapses in communication between Thomas and Colette after she married and moved away: at least a year and often more. He was the one to break the silence with pithy emails or short phone calls that ended with his saying they should do this more often. He boasted of his accomplishments: a new offshoot of his company; a condo in Hilton Head; a palatial home in Philadelphia's Garden District; a pied-à-terre in Rittenhouse Square. They talked about books they had both read, and about places she and her husband had traveled to. When she said she had loved seeing Paris again and been delighted to have retained much of the French she had become fluent in during her junior year abroad, he said he intended to study French and move to France. "France!" she said. "Why France?" Because he had been to Paris for a few days on business and liked it.

He rarely inquired about her two children. On one occasion he stopped by her Connecticut home unannounced while her husband was at work. She had answered the door wearing a sweatshirt and jeans, auburn hair pinned up with strands hanging this way and that, a baby on her hip and one tugging at her sweatshirt. He took them all out for ice cream, strolling Main Street—the youngest on his shoulders, the older between them, skipping to keep pace—as though the four of them were a unit. How easy it had been to be a family without commitment—without the messy work.

"You haven't changed a bit," he said to her much later, after seeing her Facebook page. He likened her to Dorian Gray, the narcissistic literary character who made a Faustian bargain never to age.

"He was hardly admirable!" she said.

Still, he went on to address her in each email as Dorian. She acquiesced enough to signing off with the newly given name. A frivolous fantasy she allowed him, but one for which he took full credit. That went on for several years, followed by several more of silence, except for the holiday cards they exchanged: hers always coming from herself and her husband; his addressed only to her and always signed T, as though he was still the secret admirer who had once sent her a valentine card signed T and for years thereafter denied that it had come from him.

* * *

Then, what he had been waiting well over three decades for, happened—the arrival of a holiday card minus its customary family photo: Season's Greetings from Colette alone. Her husband had passed away, she informed him when he phoned. He had been in a biking accident. He had been battling cancer and the prognosis wasn't good, so maybe the accident was a blessing in a way. The children were grown, thank goodness. Still, she was sad—so sad. Despite her attempt to be upbeat, he detected a woman who was incomplete, one with a gaping hole in her heart. Thomas vowed to make her happy.

That spring he put in an offer on an old farmhouse in Bar Harbor, Maine, sight unseen except for online photos. Who could resist Bar Harbor? It had just been designated the most desirable place in the US to visit. He would drive up for the inspection and stay at a hotel until the closing. While there, he'd see what had to be done to the house: plan to have it gutted, if need be, but probably not—Colette liked quaint. He'd fill it with antiques he picked up from yard sales along the way. But how would he transport them? He'd arrange to have them shipped; money was no object. Then he'd call her and tell her about it, text her photos, plan to have her visit. And she'd never leave. The prospect of semi-retirement had presented itself: most of his business was now done virtually anyway, and he had plenty of assets to cover his sisters' needs.

All was going swimmingly, until he realized that he had overestimated his stamina and his ability to drive long distances. He had just made it over the Maine border when his eyelids grew heavy and he had to pull off onto the shoulder and scroll his cell phone for lodging. Luckily, his inspection wasn't scheduled until midafternoon the following day. Although there was a decent-looking motel five miles ahead, he chose a romantic B and B off the beaten path, one that would have met Colette's approval. The place was so remote he lost cell service trying to find it, and somehow, an hour later, he stood at its door barely able to remain on his feet.

* * *

In the morning he was awakened by a gentle knock at his door. "If you're done with that menu, you can slip it under here," a voice with a distinct New England accent devoid of *R*'s suggested.

Thomas had been too tired to notice the menu on the small oak writing desk the night before. He sprang out of bed and checked his preferences: orange juice, French toast and bacon, black coffee, and a croissant he'd take with him for the drive, and slid the menu under the door to the man in the hallway.

He showered in the upgraded glass-and-tile stall, using certain amenities offered in a wicker basket. In the dining room he found his host, a tall gentleman on the frail side, the way slender men get when they reach seventy. Thomas was glad he was still muscular, although lately he had tended to put on weight, especially in his midsection, particularly when he frequented too many

Eagles games and drank too much beer and ate too many Philly cheesesteaks.

His host placed a French press on the table and told Thomas to wait five minutes before he engaged the press. Did he want sugar? Yes? Good! Not another health nut from the big city, his smile indicated, as he left and returned with a delicate blue-and-gold-rimmed china sugar bowl and silver spoon.

"No other guests," the man said.

He pulled out a chair and made himself comfortable at the perfectly set table with a tablecloth and matching napkins, a holder for toast like the ones Thomas had seen in Scotland, a small crystal pitcher of warm maple syrup, and an unlabeled jar of what looked like strawberry jam but what turned out to be tart cherry that came from the trees in his host's backyard.

"For the record, I'm Arthur," he said, extending his hand. "I told you last night, but I doubt you remember."

"Thomas."

"I know."

"Of course, you do." Thomas cleared his throat and they both smiled. "Aren't you eating?"

"Oh, no, no," Arthur said. "Had my breakfast. I'm used to getting up with the crows. Ever since my wife died last year, I get up even earlier."

"I'm sorry," Thomas said, pushing down on the knob of the French press, feeling a little odd eating with this guy—arms folded, legs crossed—observing him.

"Thank you." Arthur seemed appreciative of the condolences that Thomas thought he would be tired of hearing by this time. And while Arthur might not have been hungry for breakfast, he apparently was for company. It had been a severe winter in the Northeast—even Thomas knew this—and spring had yet to show its true face. Visitors must have been scarce.

"Try the jam," Arthur said. "Won't be any more after this batch. The wife made it. I suppose I could always pick up some homemade jelly from the country store."

"Nice place you have here," Thomas said, taking in the floral wallpaper and crisp café curtains hanging from a fat brass rail. Colette would have liked the antique sidebar that held a three-tiered cake stand filled with cookies, a pitcher of ice water, an electric tea kettle with an ample selection of tea, and a vintage baker's rack with potted plants on one shelf and colorful linens stacked on another.

"It's all Joann—my wife," Arthur said.

Thomas picked out a croissant from a cloth-lined basket, slathered it with the jam, and took a bite. "Very good!" He felt obligated to comment on the jam. "How long have you been here?"

Thomas was surprised to learn that they had only owned the B and B for two years before Arthur's wife became ill. It had been her dream to retire and move nearer to their son and grandchild. This was to have been a fun second career. "But the best laid plans," Arthur said. He wasn't sure how much longer he could go on running the place by himself. But he didn't stop there. He told Thomas how they'd met in grade school and married soon after high school. He had been an electrician and his wife a nurse. They had three sons, but only one was still in New England—here—where the B and B was. He missed the others. Only got to see them once or twice a year.

"So, you knew in high school, huh," Thomas said.

"Hell, I knew in fourth grade! Jojo was always the one."

Thomas smiled and shook his head in admiration. "No second thoughts? No desire to—you know—play the field?"

"Nothing more than an easily dispelled notion." Arthur smiled and winked.

Now they were talking like two women who'd just met, and not like men, who in that situation tended to keep their conversation limited to sports, cars, and traffic, if they spoke at all.

"How about you, Thomas?" Arthur was too courteous to ask him if he was married or ever had been, despite his bare ring finger. Not all men wore wedding bands.

"Single."

Arthur nodded, as though Thomas didn't look like a man anyone would marry.

"I was married once—for a very short time. Didn't go well," Thomas said, wanting Arthur to know.

"Too bad, but I guess things work out for the best."

"Maybe."

Arthur stared at his guest as though he knew there was a lot more to the story. Thomas suspected the man would have given anything to have had more time—however short—with his own wife.

"So where you headed, if you don't mind my asking?" Arthur said.

"Bar Harbor."

"I'm from downtown Bar Harbor. A city boy born and bred," he said proudly.

Thomas snorted, aware that Bar Harbor's population numbered, at most, five thousand. He instantly regretted it, the way he regretted a lot of things lately.

Arthur's cold stare indicated he hadn't missed the affront. "Guess you're on your way to the park." After all, what would a pathetic guy all alone do in a small town? He had to be intending to hike or bike in Acadia, Thomas knew the innkeeper must be thinking. When he told Arthur about the house and about buying it sight unseen, Arthur was taken aback. He showed Arthur the photos on Zillow, and Arthur smiled again.

"Old Parson Watson's place," Arthur said.

"You know it?"

"Yeah, I know it." Arthur laughed. "Bar Harbor's as big as a fly on a clown's nose. But you already know that. They'll be calling your house the Watson place even after you've been there fifty years." He picked up Thomas's empty juice glass and placed it in the center of the table. "The Watson's place—*your* place," he said. Then he moved the sugar bowl six inches southeast. "*My* old place."

"What's the scale?" Thomas asked.

"About a block to an inch."

"What's it like?" Thomas was anxious to know.

"Let's say everybody knows everyone's business."

"No, I mean the house." It was the house he'd have to sell Colette on, not Maine.

"Watson kept it up as much as most do. Wife was a nice lady. I believe she passed several years ago. I'm sure it needs work. Old houses always do. Not your cup of tea if you're the turnkey type. Depends on your taste—and your purse."

"Not mine. Colette's. Taste, that is."

"And she's—"

"My whole reason for coming up here. For everything." And so, just as Arthur had done, Thomas began to talk. He told Arthur how he and Colette had met. About his ex-wife. About his sisters. About Colette's husband having recently died. He even told him about the three *S*'s with a certain amount of pride. It felt good to unload to another man. Arthur nodded, listening intently, barely cracking a smile.

"And you didn't ask her to marry you because—"

"Stupid, I guess," he said, offering the same excuse he had given Colette. The only excuse he had come to own. "I made a mistake."

"What does she think about the house?"

"Oh, she doesn't know about any of this," he said, melancholy transformed into euphoria. "I haven't seen her in a very long time. It's a surprise! I've taken care of everything."

"You don't say." Arthur's tone conveyed wariness.

Thomas's cell phone rang; he fished it out of his pocket. An associate needed advice on a potential client. "Give him the whole enchilada. You know the playbook. Whatever he needs, we can give him. And whatever it costs, he'll find the money."

"Problems?" Arthur asked.

"Nah. This is the easy stuff. Wow!" he said, noting the time. "Looks like I'd better get going. Listen, I've really enjoyed talking with you, Arthur. If you need any marketing advice, don't hesitate to get in touch." He took a card out of his wallet.

"I think I'm small potatoes for you."

"No such thing. We can work wonders. We'll have your little B and B on steroids if you know what I mean."

"Think I do."

"What about the Grand Hotel? That's where I'm staying until the closing."

"She'll suit you just fine."

"I'll go up and get my things and be on my way. So, how long a trip am I looking at?"

"Oh, a good three and a half, barring mishaps."

"No mishaps. I'm sailing a clear path now, Arthur." Surely, having shared such intimacies, the meaning of his last statement had been understood.

An upbeat Thomas, taking several steps at a time, headed back up to his room. He returned to the desk within minutes and handed Arthur his credit card. "By the way, how's the reception from here on?" he asked.

"Spotty," Arthur said. "We can put a man on the moon, but we can't manage to provide decent cell service."

"Maybe you'd better give me directions, just in case. I don't want to get lost again. Don't want to be late to my appointment. Can't miss this one. This is my chance, Arthur," he said more soberly to convince the innkeeper. "Got it all figured out, how to get and keep her now. Got it right this time."

Arthur handed back the card he had just run through the reader and Thomas took in the man. Gentle Arthur, who had listened attentively, who Thomas had seemingly entertained or at least made happy for a short while, appeared to have grown despondent. Perhaps because his only guest was departing, and the widower wasn't eager to find himself alone again. Or perhaps— Thomas pushed away the thought—he felt pity for Thomas: for his missed opportunities, his blunders, his myopic view of life, his solitude.

"Why, Thomas, I thought you'd have figured it out by now. Smart guy like you."

"Figured out what?" Let it be a glitch in his travel plans: he hadn't taken the time to map out his route. Perhaps he'd miscalculated the timing. Oh, please let it be.

"Thomas," the benevolent innkeeper, taking in those twinkling green eyes now laden with apprehension, said, "you can't get there from here."

Holway Street

There are more people than usual dotting the beach today, even though it's only spring. Most of the part-timers who claim they're Cape Codders because they summer here have normally long ago retreated to their permanent residences in New York or Jersey or Boston. But this year is different. The pandemic has driven them indoors and away from crowds, boredom and claustrophobia sending many scurrying earlier than usual, in minivans packed to the hilt, to sequester on the Cape and other less populated towns along the Eastern Seaboard. They are the fortunate ones who own a second home or have the means to rent one. Those for whom there is still no school for children to return to, no office at which to work, the bundled-up souls who have dotted the glistening sand like winter campers. The lucky ones—the nonessential: suddenly everyone wishes to be nonessential.

I've always felt nonessential, and in no way fortunate, because the way I relate to others has always been different. That's why the isolation imposed by the pandemic isn't a hardship on me.

* * *

My father stopped by my boat repair shop this morning, wearing his signature baggy jeans and T-shirt, the once-chestnut and now-silver hair curling around his ears, the same handlebar mustache reaching up toward cheeks so sunburned from overexposure they resemble the tanned leather he now uses to make belts and man bags and other items—some practical, like wallets, others use-less, like medieval change pouches—that he sells to local stores. He refuses to put his wares on the Internet. His body has never changed, though he claims he's losing muscle mass. It's all in your head, I tell him—the muscle mass, that is. He laughs. I like it when he laughs.

He's always looked the same to me: tall, trim, and slim. He says when he was in the Coast Guard here at the station in Chatham, he was all bulk, bench-pressed a hundred and eighty-five pounds. And he was smart: had top security clearance because he controlled the teletypes in the days when everything came out on paper. He had access to all that stuff. Everything was ship-to-shore in the six-ties and seventies. No cell phones back then. He was a third-grade officer. At the fourth level he'd have been in charge, but he stopped at three, saying he already had top security clearance without the headaches. Why would he go to four? If something happened, he'd have been at fault. As a boy, I wished he'd gone to four—like my classmate Johnny's father. Seemed everyone worked for the Coast Guard, and guys not nearly as smart as my dad had gone on to four. "My dad's the boss of your dad," Johnny liked to say when we were in grade school, as though that made Johnny the boss of me. These were the things kids talked about, the things that mattered. Maybe it was the thing that made my dad so quiet. Maybe he didn't want to talk about it because he regretted it, or maybe because it never mattered to him. He wasn't thinking about what the effect might be on me.

He owns the whole side of the yard in the industrial park where I work, and all the bays in it: the auto body shops, the rubbish removal, the fish and lobster company, the sheet metal works. All the bays except mine: I bought that from him and own it free and clear. My granddad was smart to buy up pieces little by little when the land was cheap. I never knew any of that or I'd have thrown it back at Johnny: My dad doesn't *have* to go to four, I could have said. But that's your granddad's land, Johnny would have shot back at me, probably feeling unsure about his own father—another thing

I wouldn't have recognized back then. Someday I'll own it all—manage it like my dad—I could have said to Johnny.

Is it fair to rely on somebody else's ambition? All my grand-dad wanted for his son was to have him take over when he was gone: family was family, no matter how the property had been acquired, no matter what my father did for a living until then. It's all about family, my father continues to say. I think he adopted that philosophy when he was a boy and his parents sent him to his father's relatives in South Philly every summer. I can't imagine being away from the Cape in summer, but my dad says they were some of the best days: hanging around on the city streets, playing stickball with his summer friends, making out with girls at the local schoolyard, big Sunday dinners with his cousins and aunts and uncles in a cramped apartment. "Italians are tight," he says. "Remember that." But we never see that side of the family anymore: they've all moved on to towns and cities all over the country. I guess I'm "tight" with some of my cousins here on the Cape, my mother's Irish and English family—the plain side, was how I used to refer to them when other kids asked me what I was. My dad's Italian, my mom's just plain, I'd say. Still, as much as I enjoy my cousins, I like to be alone. That's why I work alone. I live alone. To convince my dad that I've come around to behaving like other guys my age, I tell him there's a family hanging somewhere in the future for me, but frankly, at thirty-nine, I just don't see it. Sometimes, I have to confess, I think I'm punishing him for not going on to four.

"What's happening?" I asked my dad, who remained at the entrance, not daring to come closer because Marlene—thin as a pencil in her black yoga pants, her pink hair looking like its eraser in a topknot—was standing midway between us, properly distanced. And because he wasn't wearing his new fashion statement, the black mask that makes him look like Zorro's father.

"I made these this morning," Marlene said, motioning to a plate of chocolate chip cookies she'd just placed on my table saw, the only cleared surface available. "Have some."

Dad smiled, a glimmer of hope tickling his mustache. He's always wanted to believe there's more between me and Marlene than a plate of cookies. "A little too early for me to take in sugar," he said. "Once I start, I'll never stop. But I'm sure Colin will have polished them off before lunchtime."

I've told him Marlene doesn't like me that way—we're just friends. No one would marry me. But he says any man can get married if he wants. He's not so sure about women, though. He thinks they can if they're willing to settle. When I was around five, the subject never concerned me: I figured, like my father, I'd just marry my mother if I had to marry at all. But that's beside the point. I like things the way they are: Marlene six feet away, and my father another six feet.

"So, what's up?" I asked him again, to take his mind off Marlene, who was leaving to change into her drab gray pantsuit. She's been called back to work at the bank after a brief furlough due to the pandemic.

"Same old thing," he answered. "You said you got the pull start on order for me?"

"It should be here this week."

"Okay. So when you get that, you'll take a look at the motor and check out the sharp edges," he said, meaning the propeller that may have been dinged up on a rock or in the shallows.

"Yeah. I wanna get this one back together for you first and then I'll take care of it." I mean the engine I'm working on as we speak.

"Okay."

"Don't worry. I'm gonna make sure it's not sharp. I'll take a file to it or something."

He knows I'll get it back to him all shipshape, yet he never fails to mention the details he thinks I might overlook.

"All right. Cool. Call your mother sometime."

"I do."

"Call more. Do a drive-by."

"Okay." I laughed and shook my head. *You* never called her when you were working, I wanted to say.

My dad was raised on the Cape because my granddad, who was also in the Coast Guard, wanted a quieter place to live than Philly. And despite Dad's summers in Philly, he turned out to be more like my mom's seafaring family: he even looks like them, tanned and craggy, with his emotion in check like a ship model that's folded up and ready for the bottle. And just like that ship springs to life when its string is pulled, my dad comes to life, but only once or twice a year, when something like a Red Sox big win uncorks him. You don't know what it was like living with *the curse*, he'd say, living without hope of them ever taking the Series, us being the underdogs year after year. I tell him I do remember some of that: being made fun of by the Yankees and their fans' goddamn Curse of the Bambino signs, invoking Babe Ruth to take revenge on the Sox for having traded him to them. "Nah, you don't really know," he says. He's a crusty New Englander, all right.

My mom, on the other hand, can fool you. She'll rattle on nonstop about this or that, her even tone like taffy being pulled. She would have been a good presidential press secretary, someone who can go on and on about anything—nothing—just to shut up the reporters. That's my mom: sweet yet raspy, rambling away until you've lost the gist of the story and just want to go get a drink or take a piss. At least that's how I feel. But inside that chatterer there's a backbone like a steel girder, a woman who would hold my hand to the fire for what seemed like an eternity if I crossed her or failed to live up to her expectations for what I considered the most trivial matters. I never learned how she felt about Dad not going on to four, but I can bet she didn't like it. When I think of it that way, I'm glad he stuck to his guns.

Other people find my mother charming, with her curly gray hair and hazel eyes. She used to be a brunette, but I can hardly remember her that way: women on the Cape don't dye their hair and they never wear hats even in the dead of winter. There's a sea of gray and white heads, like the crests of ocean waves, in church or at a concert or town meeting. She used to work at the Coast Guard station just like her mother, who worked the switchboard in the nineteen forties, plugging cables into the right holes, listening to other people's conversations, chatting away at the same time to her own party. Only my mother sat at a Wang computer, although she would have preferred the switchboard so she could eavesdrop. When I thought about marrying her when I was a kid, I figured I'd just get earplugs. I'm a practical kind of guy.

The pandemic is killing my mom, not because she's got COVID, but because she can't hang around the post office or at the knitting shop with her friends, crocheting baby clothes for the needy or playing mah-jongg and chatting about how much better things were when FDR was president, even though she wasn't alive then and there was a world war raging. The long-ago past has an allure, always signaling it was the best of times, even when it was the worst. And now she's troubled by knitting all alone and delivering meals she leaves on doorsteps without the customary hug or handshake. She says texting doesn't do it for her, besides, it costs too much. I tell her she can get unlimited data, but she doesn't believe me, says there must be a catch. There is, I tell her, but for her it would be worth it. She brushes my advice aside, as always. She takes long walks on the beach with her best friend, Ellie, keeping masked and properly distanced, widening the gap for the occasional runner they encounter. I like Ellie, but I think she's going deaf, which works well for my mom.

My mom was the first mother on Holway Street to run out of the house with a blanket to wrap around an injured child after hearing the sound of screeching brakes. My dad, methodically and without so much as a word to us or the neighbors, would leave the house and go from driveway to driveway with his plow attached to his pickup after one of the Cape's infrequent snowstorms. Their do-gooding embarrassed me. Why couldn't they just mind their own business? They're not that nice deep down, I wanted to say. At least not to me. But that wasn't true: they were just parents who were different from me, the way I was different from other kids. Colin's shy, my mother used to offer as an excuse for my silence and sullenness around grown-ups, my refusal to play with their kids.

"Bashful" was another word she used to describe me, as though it were some congenital disease and not a disorder that plagued me. I cringed when people responded with "Like father, like son," trying to make me normal—or my father abnormal. I cringed when I was small because I was ashamed of Dad; I cringed as I got older because I felt I wasn't as good as he was.

That was when we lived on Holway Street—the best place to be—fifty feet from the ocean. My dad says he never slept so well as when we lived there. You could see the lighthouse from my upstairs window; you could hear the ocean at the end of the street. All the locals lived by the water then. I spent every free moment on the beach or snorkeling and discovering odds and ends: silverware, broken plates, and thermoses I liked to imagine had come from old ships and hotels, but maybe had been discarded by beachgoers. It was idyllic. "In, buddy." I can still hear my father's protective bellow while he motioned with an outstretched arm for me to come to shore at dinnertime. I could drive a dune buggy from morning until night along the beach and never run over the same grain of sand twice. I could get lost there—really be alone. Those were the best days.

"Why did your family leave Holway Street?" Marlene asked me one day when the reality of the pandemic was starting to hit and we were on the cusp of closing down and going remote. She would have called it a date. I guess it was: a date between two friends who had grown up on the same street, gone to the same schools, swum in the same waters, had sex from time to time.

"You know why," I said. "Same reason you're living way out on Payton Road now and you need to drive to the beach. We got flooded out during the hurricane. Remember? Maybe you don't remember. You were only a kid. I was a lot older than you."

"Not that much. It just mattered more then." She frowned, turning her cute lower lip inside out. "But I do remember. Hurricane Bob. We had no choice but to go."

"By the time we wanted to come back into town," I said, "our landlords had sold out to all those wealthy dot-com people who gobbled up property for pennies. Then came the fancy stores and restaurants—knocking down our old haunts and bringing in all that glam construction, raising the price of homes that would barely be occupied. And there we were, kiddo, living on the *outskirts* of town because no townie could afford to live *in* it. And now they want to stay full-time because of the virus and keep their dune buggies and Camaros in my dad's bays while their BMWs are sitting in their garages. They got *their* gas pumps, *their* little setup while they work on their cars and party. It's an *industrial* park, not an amusement park! That shit shouldn't be allowed. Something's wrong with that picture, don't you think?" I enjoyed explaining stuff to Marlene, telling her things she didn't know or remember.

"Blame it on Bob."

"Yeah." I laughed. "I guess we can blame it on Bob. But as much as I complain, there's another side: I make money off them, fixing their boats. They like coming to me."

"Because they can trust you."

"They don't really know me."

"They know you enough, Colin. They may even like you." She cups my chin as though I'm a little boy and she's the grown-up; I try hard not to pull away. I like the way she smells. Smells are important, and I'm wondering if I should have put on some of that aftershave my mother gave me for Christmas last year that I've never opened.

"My old house is a fancy B and B now," she says.

"Mine too."

"Blame it on Bob," we say in unison.

"Some of the houses that need work are going for cheap again," she says. "People just want turnkey places to hide in during this pandemic. My friend Kayley and her boyfriend just bought one. You ever think of buying? I mean, don't you want your own place?"

"I got my own place. I own my bay. Free and clear."

"I mean a house. You can't raise a family in a bay in an industrial park."

"Who says I want a family? Besides, I live in a house," I say. "What do you think this is?"

"But you rent it. And only a few rooms of it."

"What are you getting at, Marlene? You only own a condo big enough for you and your cat."

She lowered her head for a while. When she lifted it, she looked at me as though she was looking for somebody who wasn't there.

"Nothing. I'm getting at nothing, it seems. *We're* getting at nothing." She got up to find her sweater and bag.

"You wanna stay the night?" I had the audacity to ask.

"No, Colin. Not tonight."

"They closed the bank to customers today. You working the drive-through tomorrow?"

"No, Colin." She sounded as exasperated as my mother used to when I'd ask a stupid question she'd answered a thousand times before. "I'm on furlough—with the bank and with *you*."

We didn't see each other for a few months after that, until this morning, when she came into the shop with the chocolate chip cookies. It wasn't an apology; Marlene knows she doesn't owe me one. It was a lifeline—an anchor she threw out, and maybe for the last time. My dad's appearance threw me another anchor, saving me from having to make a decision: grab onto Marlene's anchor or lose it forever. I don't know why she cares about me. Marlene is smart, so smart that the bank, for all its stuffiness, lets her work there despite her pink hair.

* * *

This afternoon I'm making a house call. I don't particularly like house calls if the owners are home, but I'm disappointed when I don't find the owners at this one. The boat with the motor I need to tune up for the season is in the front yard. Everything I can possibly need is beside it in my pickup: cardboard cartons, plastic tubs, metal pails, and toolboxes; the rest of the stuff—like my high boots and jumper cables, wipes, plastic drop cloths, gallons of oil, spray cans of lubricant—is there too, all in order: my shop away from shop. My mom says I never kept my bedroom in order. My tools are in *my* order: I can put my finger on anything with my eyes closed. But I don't jump right into fixing their outboard motor. I take in what's happening on this tree-shaded property.

Looks as though they're at it again: there's a wheelbarrow on its side, bags of mulch and cedar chips, plastic pails of tree cuttings, and clay bowls filled with colored stones the size of cranberries all waiting to add to the organized chaos the owners have created— their unique way of decorating and landscaping their yard. An old clawfoot bathtub, painted red on the outside, with pink and white geraniums growing in a window box inside of it, sits on a bed of sea glass. A mermaid hangs on a wooden stockade fence next to a small randomly placed sign that reads: LIVE! The sign is new and would usually give me the urge to grab a beer and go fishing, but today it shouts out a more sober definition of survival.

In the far corner of the yard, almost behind the house, is a two-foot-high stump with a large Buddha sitting on top of it. I feel compelled to greet the Buddha, whose silence and stillness attracts me. His eyes are closed, as though he chooses not to see me or be distracted by anything—or maybe they're open and he has no eyeballs. I don't know enough about Buddhism, except that it's about inner peace and gentleness—maybe even forgiveness. Across from the Buddha there's a series of concrete blocks painted in pastel blues and lavenders with red, white, and blue buoys sitting on top like a flock of ducks in a row—the only semblance of order amid a folded card table, a window screen, a metal dolly propped against the trunks of tall pines. Chain-link fencing forms a small three-sided shelter. But for what purpose, if you can escape from the fourth side? Wooden stepladders, hoes, rakes, shovels, and spades hang on another section of fencing, as though the tools are being hidden—but again, from what? Because it's all out there for every-one to see. All disorderly, yet very orderly in my eyes.

I head down the bluestone steps, like Alice tumbling down the rabbit hole. On the patio made of crushed clamshells there's a glass table with lobster traps for its base. The Adirondack chairs—each a different brightly painted color—seem too common among the bird feeders, wagon wheels, and glittering wire-and-mesh fairies hanging on the natural surrounding wall of rock and soil. But nothing seems out of place in this oasis where everything is out of place. A winding path of white stones is studded with clumps of blue and magenta hydrangeas. Water trickles from a spiraling stone fountain. A small bench fashioned from slabs of granite holds another Buddha, a black one that's adorned with a necklace of strategically placed turquoise stones. A scallop shell sits on top like a lace chapel veil my grandmother used to pin to her hair when she went to church. More fountains. Large patches of Montauk daisies, Queen Anne's lace, and Russian sage.

I stand before the Buddha, enjoying the solitude among the disarray, and it's hard to go back to work because I want to stay and observe every little pebble, every hue of color, every fairy's wing, envisioning times past and those to come, until a lightness carries me over the waves like a raft at sea and I lose track of the time, as I often do, and find myself back on Holway Street.

Marlene's family lived two doors down from us. Her mom managed what was the only guesthouse there at the time. She didn't own it; just managed it, cleaned it, and served the breakfast. That was the first place my dad would clear the snow from before he started down the street. He knew Marlene's mother had it tough enough with three kids and no husband. Marlene liked hanging around me—just like now. Showing up at our back door on Saturday mornings, cute as a button, my mother would say, with her pigtails, big brown eyes, those skinny legs, and a husky voice way too mature for her age, one that startled you. We invited her in most days, and she'd make a beeline for me, wanting to know what I was doing then and for the rest of the day, asking if she could tag along. She liked to go clamming on rainy days. She didn't care that I didn't talk to her much. She was my only friend. Her mom liked her going with me on those days too, so that one of her kids would be occupied and out of the house; she also liked the clams Marlene would bring back for chowder. It was easy to be with Marlene's family because their dad had been gone for so long nobody ever compared *their* dad to *my* dad. They just loved *mine*.

Marlene cried when she saw us pack up and move, but it was my dad who had cried first. He didn't know, but I'd seen him the night before, while we were walking on the beach—the sky lit up by a full moon—while my mom was flitting around the house, taking charge of the move, all excited about the newly built home the government was subsidizing: more space for more antiques she could collect, more land for a garden. When I looked over at him (I was nearly his height by then), I saw his eyes all watery, his mustache wet and glistening, and it frightened me. That's when he told me he was sorry we had to go.

"We can live in the bays," I had said, just like I'd told Marlene on our date. "Granddad will let us."

He laughed.

"We can come back," I said, "when everything's all cleaned up. We can build a new house."

"Your mom won't want to come back," he said, sharing the fact of a disagreement between them that I didn't appreciate at the time.

"Why does she have to get her way? It's not fair."

"Happy wife, happy life," he said, resigned.

"You don't seem happy," I said, hating my mother for it.

I remember thinking that maybe if Dad had gone to fourth, we'd have had enough money to own our house on Holway Street—and we could have rebuilt and not moved, and my mother wouldn't have gotten her way. I remember thinking that maybe my dad was finally regretting not having gone to fourth, too.

I started seeing Marlene a few years ago. She'd begun dropping by my bay just the way she used to come to our kitchen door, to talk while I worked. Only instead of my mother giving her some treat every now and then, she was the one who brought the goodies. I've grown to like conversing with Marlene: maybe it's because I like the deep mellow tone of a voice you still don't expect to come out of such a petite body, or that scent she wears, or because I've known her since she was a tot, which makes her less intimidating than other women. But there's only so long before two adults can hang out before they hook up. I figured we'd just stay the way we were until Marlene found someone else—someone more worthy of her. What were you thinking? Mr. Buddha asks. Eyeless Buddha, who is anything but blind. Who knows that if you blink, you can miss it all.

The screen door slams shut like a shot from a rifle, or more like the reveille my dad used to play with his bugle every morning to wake me up. While I groaned like hell about it, deep down I thought it was amusing, laughing into my pillow because my dad laughed after he'd done it. We both laughed, the window on Holway Street wide open, the curtain waving outside like a sail taken by the wind. As I said before, I like it when he laughs, even at my expense. I like it when he's happy.

When I look up from the patio, a barefoot woman in khaki shorts is standing there, smiling: long white muscular legs speckled with a few red spider veins, and gray hair pulled into a ponytail.

"Didn't think you were home, Linda. Didn't see your vehicle."

"Oh, Ed's brought it to the shop for tires and his is already in the shop. Saved me the trip," she says, still smiling. She has a large, intimidating mouth like Julia Roberts and isn't wearing a surgical mask to hide it, but neither am I. Having to maintain the space between us works for me because it's embarrassment that keeps my clay legs firmly planted on the ground. That's when she realizes about the mask.

"I forgot my mask! Do you mind? I can run in and get one."

"That's okay, Linda," I say, still appearing to be socially distancing. Actually, I *am* "socially" distancing because I'm kind of nervous around Linda, even more than I am around other people.

Linda's a potter, a poet, and a fine water skier, gardener, and guitarist. Leads meditation groups. Always smiling that big broad grin that I wonder if my mouth could ever cover if I kissed her. I also wonder sometimes how people can smile so much. They train themselves to be that way, my mother used to say. You decide to be positive—upbeat—and you, you know, put on a happy face, Colin. Come on, Colin, try. It's good to be like that, Colin; we should all try to smile more.

How can so much imperfection look so perfect? I ask myself as I take in Linda and the property. "Your workshop is perfect," Marlene told me once, and I laughed. I don't know why I laughed, because I'd spent a lot of time organizing it, and deep down I was proud. "Seriously. It's perfect for what you do, Colin. It's perfect for you." She stopped short of saying that *I* was perfect, and that's a good thing. That's what makes Marlene so honest. So smart.

"I should get to work myself. I'll have this motor in shape before Ed returns," I say to Linda, who has discovered me nowhere near the boat.

"Take your time."

Linda is about my mother's age, but I find her much more interesting and attractive than my mother. I think most people feel that way about their parents. I want to take off the silly fishing hat I'm wearing that protects my fair skin from the sun and makes me look like a geek. But that would be too obvious.

"Can I get you something to drink? Hot already for this time of year."

"Yup. She's gonna be a scorcher," I say, but that's an exaggeration. "I'm all set," I then tell her, anticipating the large thermos of iced tea I have in my pickup.

"You sure? You'll be sorry. It's fresh-squeezed lemonade."

"I'm good, Linda. Thank you."

I should ask how her daughter Stacie, who lives in Boston, is. We went to school together, though we were never friendly. I wasn't friendly with anyone. But I know I should ask.

"How's Stacie?" I manage to say it without making eye contact.

"Stressful time for her. We haven't seen her since the pandemic took hold—can't, of course. She worries about being around us. She and her husband split up, you know, on top of that." She shrugs.

"I didn't know."

"It'll be okay. It'll *all* be okay," Linda says to assure me, this time with a half-smile I catch because I've turned to face her. "We all get stuck in the mud, Colin. That's what fear does: it immobilizes. It inhibits vulnerability." She smiles again, only this time her

eyebrows go up as if to say, "Are you really listening? I have something important to tell you. Did you get it?"

Now I'm spinning with an exciting yet painful adrenaline rush
of discovery, like I'm skiing down a mountain, about to lose control.
I want to just fall, throw myself on the ground and end it, but she
keeps at it.

"People who get discouraged and stop persevering get worn
down. Don't let fear ever stop you. It's all about balance: pushing
and avoidance. If you're feeling discouraged, you're losing perse-
verance and going into pushing. When you're impatient you push,
when you push, you're discouraged. If you sustain your own balance,
other people have to deal with theirs."

I'm wondering if she weeps on account of her own anguish as
easily as she tunes in to someone else's demons; if she listens with
as much attention to Stacie as she does to people who are practi-
cally strangers. I think about what it must have been like for Stacie,
growing up with a mother like her, without an escape route out of
her own mind.

"Your dad was singing your praises to Ed the other day," she
says.

"Maybe Ed was singing to my dad."

"No, I said it right the first time. He's proud of you, Colin—
your business. Of what you've accomplished." She follows this up
with that big toothy grin and turns to walk toward the house to
go write poetry or squeeze more lemons or just get away from me.
Then she does an about-face.

"You can come whenever you'd like," she says.

I'm a little surprised and don't quite know how to take that. I'm
a little happy, too.

"To the meditation garden," she says. "Any time, Colin. It's like
the ocean, only maybe better. Good for the soul. And if you ever
want to sit in on a Zoom class—no pressure." And with that she
goes into the house, careful not to let the screen door slam this time.

I start working on the boat's motor, thinking about how—like
my dad—I enjoy what I do, taking a drill and a wire brush to the

corrosion and salt buildup, making a shrill sound ten times as loud as a dentist's drill and hoping it isn't bothering Linda, even though I know it's not. At this time, on this day, in this spot, Linda knows, and I know, the sound is perfect.

* * *

I was just finishing up at Linda and Ed's, about to head out and pick up some takeout from Big Al's Barbecue for an early dinner. I thought I'd take it over to Marlene's if she was in the mood, and we could eat it in the small yard behind her condo or maybe even take it to an empty area on the beach with the CDC-recommended amount of space between us. I've been missing Marlene. I think things can be better between us. I'd like to be better than I am.

I went to text her when she beat me to it with a call. My dad had been sitting at the drive-through window of the bank, having as much of a conversation with her as he could, considering the line of cars behind him, when he kind of went weird on her: his speech slurring, as though he'd slipped into some deep trance. Marlene called 911 even before she alerted the manager. After the ambulance left for Hyannis with my father, Marlene asked another teller to relieve her so she could drive over to my parents'. That's where I find her and my mother now, on the deck out back. My mother is wrapped in one of my father's old flannel work shirts, standing with her arms folded, nervously tapping one foot; Marlene—six feet away—is seated at a peeling white-wicker table that has two glasses and a pitcher of water on it. None of us are wearing masks. I haven't been inside my parents' house for over three months.

"I can't even be with him," my mother says, mouth tense, as I run up the wooden steps and then stop short before getting too close to her—to the look, the pitiful one of impossible longing that dares me to give more than I'm capable of giving because she has never shown me how. "They won't let me into the hospital." Her voice cracks and I steel myself in preparation: I don't ever remember seeing her cry, unless she was what she liked to call "shit-faced" at some barbecue or holiday and laughing until, according to her, she almost "wet her pants" at some joke one of her inebriated siblings had told. Sure enough, she catches herself and regains her composure.

I stand there taking in my mother: oddly isolated in the outdoors, not surrounded by her treasured antique furniture and busy carpets, her baskets overflowing with colorful yarn, her gleaming copper pots; a brittle figure unanchored, about to be swept off by the slightest breeze.

"I'm there, Mom," I say, meaning I'll drive up-Cape to Hyannis—the big city, as we call it—as fast as I can.

"I said they won't let you in, Colin," she says firmly. *Don't you understand, Colin. Don't you ever understand?* I know she's thinking. "Goddamn pandemic!"

"I'm going anyway," I say, refusing to let her tell me what to do.

"The closest you'll get is the parking lot," Marlene says, echoing her warning. Despite the distress I'm feeling—the need to stay focused—it strikes me how much her presence grounds me.

My mother's tightly sealed lips are keeping any hint of weakness from escaping. Fuck it, I tell myself and inch nearer to her, and then nearer still, until we're standing side by side and I force myself to put my arm around her, ready and waiting for the tension in her shoulders to surrender.

* * *

It's a while before they use my dad's cell phone to call with FaceTime. We're still on the deck, where it's growing colder and getting dark, all three of us having broken the rules and moved a little closer to one another. I hold my mom's phone at arm's length, maneuvering it so we're both in the picture. Someone—a nurse or orderly—is holding dad's. We see him lying on the raised mattress, propped up with pillows and oxygen tubes in his nostrils, IVs in his arms, wearing a wrinkled hospital gown. He's worn looking, white as a ghost, mouth askew.

"You look good, Dad!" I say.

He tries to laugh, but his faint smile is hidden not by his black mask or bushy mustache but by the stroke that's frozen one side of his face. His half-closed blue eyes are the same, and I marvel at how easy it is to read the mind of this man of few words. I fear that if I close my own eyes, like Buddha, I'll miss something. *Wiseass, I'm sorry to be such a bother,* he says. *Take care of your mother. And, by the way, wiseass, don't tell her that I'm frightened,* he silently implores. I want to crawl onto the bed to lie beside him and force that twisted mouth into a straight-out grin.

"I went over to Holway Street today," I tell him. "You should see what's going down. You and me, we'll check it out soon. Take a walk on the beach. It's gonna be okay, Dad. It'll all be okay. Right, Mom?" I try to coax some positivity out of her the way Linda might do.

But my mother—now unrecognizable—just stares at him as though she's undergone a stroke of her own, as though in disbelief that her husband is lying helpless in a hospital bed and the man standing so close to her, behaving in such an unfamiliar fashion, is her son.

Cocullo

I learned at an early age that voices carry. Over grassy town commons and busy boulevards. Through plaster walls of old row houses and quaint B and Bs. Through the cinderblock and supposedly soundproof construction of luxury hotels and modern-day condominiums. Voices carry.

"George, you old fart, get off the couch and wash the windows!" the woman across the street yelled to her husband, who answered with a "Fuck off!" or "Go to hell." That was when I lived with my grandmother on the second floor of a Brooklyn brownstone. Particularly in summer the couple's voices shot out of their open windows clear as a bell. A bell that rang out expletives and bitterness and disappointment. I couldn't understand how they coexisted like that day after day.

"You make your bed, you lie in it," my grandmother said.

My parents had made their bed; they had bought a new fancy gas-guzzling car that took them to their deaths.

"At least they went together," my bereaved grandmother had said. "It's a miracle, in this world, for any couple to stay married."

The newlyweds whose uncovered shower window was separated from our bathroom window by a narrow alleyway giggled a lot. I sometimes lifted my shade for a peek, observing them in a sudsy embrace. One night I heard the woman screaming over and over for him to stop. The next morning I was sitting on my stoop, waiting for my friend to pick me up for school, when they emerged from their apartment house door into the dark cloudy day. She stood perfectly still, stone-faced in a trench coat and pair of large sunglasses, until he stepped out and, smiling with an odd satisfaction, took her hand and led the mummy-like woman away. When I told my grandmother what I had heard and seen, she said, "You make your bed, you lie in it." They must have moved out soon afterward because, like magic, they seemed to disappear.

* * *

Sander and I traveled well together. At least that's one of the ways I liked to describe our relationship, although that made it seem as though we didn't wilt like lettuce or rot like fruit. He was willing to take on new adventures and preferred to arrange our trips on his own. That way, he said, there was no one he could blame for any gripes he might have; he owned his decisions and opinions, of which he had many. *Admirable*, I thought. And I was tired of traveling alone. Of living alone. Safeguarding the investments of others and providing for their futures had propelled me onto the other side of the glass ceiling, with a big bank account but a small social life.

We hadn't met on a dating site, many of which I had long ago soured on and frankly had very little time for. I favored low-risk, secure, and tangible bets with very little guesswork involved. That's why I agreed to a blind date with a friend of a friend's cousin who had recently found himself back in the dating game. As healthy, solvent, and attractive as people can be in midlife, we appeared quite compatible on paper and in bed. For the first time that I could remember, I felt happy. No, that's not quite correct. I had been happy, even complete. Let's say I felt happier. But before Sander moved into my town house, I needed to be sure.

"You can never be sure," my friend said. "Nothing is risk-free, even in the financial world. How well does any person know another?"

I created a spreadsheet of all possible pros and cons. When the cons outnumbered the pros, I created one based on quality of life in living alone. When that failed to yield the desired outcome, I said screw it and threw caution to the wind because I also knew that, at my age, the kind of opportunity Sander represented didn't happen often.

He moved in, taking half my closet space, cluttering my kitchen counters with fancy coffeemakers and gadgets he insisted were essential, exchanging my comfy queen-sized bed for a king—claiming he was a restless sleeper—and my down comforter for a synthetic one because he was allergic to feathers. However, I was learning that certain things were—to succumb to trendy jargon—priceless, and that it was all about compromise, as my friend said. According to her, I had lived alone for too long. I had to admit that Sander made me feel equal to the other colleagues and friends who seemed to have it all.

* * *

We hadn't planned to go to Cocullo. Neither of us had ever heard of it, and it wasn't in any guidebook. I'd never even wanted to go to the Abruzzo region, but Sander said we had to see it, especially its capital L'Aquila, and that it was the next Tuscany. I told him I thought that was Umbria, but he shook his head. I'd wanted to see the lake district; Sander warned that it was still cold and damp up there.

"Trust me, I've been in Lombardy this time of year, and it's way too chilly for you. You don't want to get sick, do you?"

He was right. I did get sick often when I traveled. In Hawaii I'd caught the flu, and in Prague a terrible sinus infection. I didn't want to ruin his vacation, so I agreed to Abruzzo. As usual, Sander had been right, because I caught the sniffles on our flight and Italy was experiencing a colder than usual spring. That's why we chose to spend our first day and night at a Rome airport luxury hotel. Sander said it would help get rid of whatever bug I'd caught and not let it drag out and ruin our vacation.

"Rest is what you need," he said. "Bed rest and lots of hot liquids because"—he winked and passed his hand over his bald head as if shining an apple—"you know how I get around you and hotels, and I don't want to get sick."

He was right, as usual, about what hotel rooms did to his libido. Sometimes I felt more like a call girl than his partner when we stayed in one, and traveling did take its toll on me. I had lived a planned and orderly life, having taken pains to learn what foods were safest, how many hours of sleep I needed, and how much and what kind of exercise suited my physiology. Adjusting to another's time frame was killing me, but I was learning to be flexible and to accept advice. In short, to be taken care of. Sander was on the mark about this one: after a deep sleep and several bowls of minestrone he brought me, I managed to avoid my usual jetlag on our first day and was ready to pick up the compact rental car that barely held our luggage.

"Small is best," Sander said. "They'll think we're Europeans."

"But the car has a logo and our luggage is too obvious."

"Only when we're en route. Once we unpack at our hotels, no one will suspect us."

* * *

Sander was more than adept at locating our first destination, though L'Aquila, with its imposing castle and fountain of ninety-nine spouts overlooking the Gran Sasso mountain range, was our prime destination. He had an app on his smartphone in addition to maps to forestall any logistic mishaps. I relaxed. He did grow frustrated when he couldn't locate our small hotel in the heart of the old medieval town Sulmona, however, leaving me to spy its nondescript façade tucked away behind the piazza through a narrow passage-way. Once we stepped into the small foyer he relaxed, but I grew wary as we came face-to-face with a female mannequin dressed in what seemed a Middle Eastern costume of turquoise, red, and gold brocade. Her heavily made-up countenance—smoky deep-set eyes and bright-red lips molded in a disarming smile—seemed to imply that she knew all about the goings-on in this hotel.

"You make it," an accented voice said.

"We certainly did," Sander responded to the compact middle-aged woman at the reception desk a few feet beyond the statue.

"When you did not come yesterday, I worry. But you are here today! Welcome to Sulmona. Your room is ready."

We handed her our passports and Sander grudgingly went back to the car to fish out the rental agreement, and the license plate number she'd also requested.

"Parking is free," she said. "But only here. Be careful. The police are attentive, especially with rentals."

"Like they'll ever be able to track us down once we leave the country," Sander whispered in my ear.

She handed me a heavy skeleton key and directed us to the spiral stone staircase. The interior of the hotel was ornate and not nearly as modern as its website had led us to believe. But I'd learned from previous trips to the country that this was common in medieval Italian towns, where people preferred concealment to exposure.

We didn't unpack since we were spending only two nights in our room, with its red damask wallpaper and dark, heavily carved furniture.

"Is there a map?" Sander asked when we went back downstairs.

"Of course, *signore*." She removed a small one of the town from behind the desk and circled our location.

"Any recommendations for dinner?" I asked.

"Osteria nell'Arco," she said without hesitation. "You see it just as you pass under the archway to the piazza. You don't miss it. Is the best."

"The guidebook says Da Gino is the best," Sander said.

"You ask me, and I tell you. Osteria nell'Arco," she repeated, raising her eyebrows as if daring him to challenge her again.

"Sounds good to me!" I accepted the map, not wanting to offend our hostess.

The day was dreary but mild, as Sander had promised. The fact that there were few must-see attractions here, and therefore no other tourists, was a nice way to ease into the culture and what would have been a different century had it not been for the teenage boys kicking a soccer ball and a couple making out on a stone wall in the otherwise vacant piazza. Sander and I laughed.

"Some things never change," he said.

He put his arm around my shoulder the way the boy on the wall embraced his girlfriend and gave me a peck on the cheek. To his surprise, I turned toward him and bestowed a smacker on his lips.

"*This*," he said, "is the *real* Italy."

We wandered up and down the winding backstreets and ended up on Corso Ovidio, where the numerous candy shops could be mistaken for florists, with bouquets of the famous confections manufactured on the outskirts of town adorning their entryways. Sander bought me a spray of sugar-coated almonds wrapped in glistening, bright-orange paper that resembled flowers with shiny gold centers. Other storefront windows displayed embroidered tablecloths and napkins. I purchased a square tablecloth with poinsettias in red, green, and gold embroidered around the edges to save for the Christmas holidays, wishing my grandmother were still alive so I could give it to her.

We found the arch the signora had told us about and the restaurant. But the maître d' said we were too early, so we had to wander the town for another hour until the eatery opened its doors to us, its first customers. The cavernous, no-frills room with dingy ocher stucco walls made Sander dubious about the signora's recommendation. "Probably a relative of hers," he said as he rearranged the table setting, placing the fork on the left with the linen napkin and the spoon and knife on the right, as he often did, explaining that it was "the way we do it." The "we" meant his family. But the food proved to be as our hostess had touted. A large buffet table displayed an array of thirty dishes ranging from appetizers to desserts: a large assortment of vegetables, some of which we had never seen, grilled and delicately seasoned with tasty herbs, oils, and vinegars; tangy cheese-filled pastas in various shapes with colorful sauces; and meats and hard-boiled eggs with fragrant stuffing that melted in our mouths. Sander returned for seconds and thirds. In no time the place filled up with families—clearly the locals' choice and our good fortune.

When we returned to the hotel, the imposing make-believe lady again startled me, inviting me to linger and examine her in greater detail. Sander, however, having secured our key from the signora's son, who apparently took the evening shift at the reception desk, had a more urgent agenda and called me away.

* * *

I don't know what time it was when I heard him; there was no clock on the nightstand, and my phone was charging on the desk and out of reach. I lay perfectly still, waiting for another sound from the other side of the wall. It was a man, I concluded, and he was moaning.

"Sander." I gently nudged him. "Sander!"

"What's up?" he mumbled, displeased at being torn from a deep sleep.

"Listen."

"So?"

"I think he's sick. We should call the front desk."

Sander opened his eyes and listened more closely.

"Probably a nightmare."

My adrenaline spiked. Sander was drifting back to sleep when the man let out a deep and loud groan that jarred him back to consciousness.

"I think he's having a heart attack!" I said.

Sander smiled. "Orgasm. He just got off. Don't interfere, little girl. Leave the man to his pleasure. All quiet now." He patted my head and rolled over. "Go to sleep."

* * *

The signora was back at her post and all aflutter when we came down in the morning. We'd overslept and missed breakfast, so we'd need to get coffee at a nearby café.

"But you are in luck!" she said. "Is a special day. La Festa dei Serpari!"

We drew a blank.

"*Serpari. I serpenti.*" She made an undulating movement with her hand and arm. "*I serpenti.* You know?"

"Snakes?" I guessed at the charade.

"*Si!* Snakes! The Festa of San Domenico. In Cocullo." She grew more excited. "Hurry! It begins soon."

"Where is this place?" Sander asked.

She laid out a map of the region on the desktop and delineated the route with a pen. "Forty, forty-five minutes. I remind my son, but he has no interest. You know, is nothing new for him. You must go! But hurry!"

"I hate snakes," I said, at which the signora smiled and shook her head, assuring me that I shouldn't be frightened. Sander and I looked at each other and decided that after a quick cup of cappuccino we would give it a go.

"I can't even go into the reptile house at the zoo," I said to Sander on our ride to Cocullo.

"Oh, come on. What could it be like? Probably something like what Saint Patrick means to Ireland. Maybe he chased away the snakes at some point and they commemorate it with an annual parade or something."

We drove the narrow road leading up to the hamlet and pulled in behind a long row of parked cars. From there we continued on foot toward the small stone church at the top of the hill, not quite sure of what to expect or exactly why we were there. Carnival-style stands lined the road, their vendors hawking toys and memorabilia shaped like snakes. There were baskets of bread loaves in various serpentine shapes, or interlocking rings of snakes biting their tails with sliced almonds for scales and coffee beans for eyes.

"Gross," I said.

"Long time ago we ate real snakes on this day," one of the English-speaking vendors said. "We cook and eat. But now only bread." He laughed.

"Why?" Sander asked.

"San Domenico protect us from the bite of the snake and from"—pointing to his teeth and cupping his hand around his jaw—"*dolore.*"

"I got it. Toothaches," Sander said. "Weird."

We approached the church and were quickly drawn into the crowd. When I looked around me, I realized that everyone had at least one live snake draped around their neck or dangling from their hands. Young men held girls in tight jeans and bare midriffs with one arm while a thick brown or gray serpent slithered along the other. Toddlers in strollers delighted in long but thin ones held in tiny fists. Fat striped and speckled snakes coiled around the wrists of angelic little girls in the Abruzzo costumes of a bygone era. Gaiety and laughter abounded. And so did snakes.

"What the hell *is* this? It's disgusting!" I didn't know where to look to avoid them. My stomach turned; my skin became sweaty and prickly.

Church bells rang and everyone cheered as a procession of parishioners with their snakes streamed out of the tiny sanctuary, leading the way for what was clearly the main event: the procession featuring a statue topped with a cross. We guessed the figure must be San Domenico, who had an enormous clump of writhing snakes of various colors and patterns wrapped around him. The grinning priest held a pole with the holy image aloft for all to see and carried it to the small piazza, where throngs of ecstatic worshippers had gathered to touch the image and the reptiles.

"I need to get out of here," I said.

"Come on! It's cool." Sander led me closer to the square.

"I can't. I really can't."

"Don't be a baby." He poked me in the ribs. I felt nausea rising.

People on crutches hobbled toward the priest, vying to touch San Domenico without letting go of their supports.

"Really, Sander. I need to go."

A boy held out his fat green-and-black-spotted snake to Sander, who took it in both hands.

"Don't!" I cried and turned away. Next I felt the heavy, dry, and cold body around my bare neck and saw its head leading its body as it slithered upward—as though weightless—toward my face. I screamed. I never scream. I am a calm and controlled individual. "Get it off! Get it off!" I begged, twisting my shoulders every which way, trying to shake off the creature as its head veered closer, its body grew heavier, and the boy and Sander laughed, until I puked up my morning's cappuccino and *cornetto* in the middle of the crowded piazza and an old woman kindly handed me a linen handkerchief to wipe my mouth.

"Well, that was quite a show you put on," Sander said after we'd made our way out of the piazza and I stopped on the way to our car to pee in a smelly porta potty. "I wouldn't have expected that from you. No fangs. They have no fangs, you know," Sander said, lecturing me as we descended the dusty hillside. "The vendor who spoke English told me when you were in the john. They collect the snakes for several weeks and store them for two more, feeding them mice and eggs. At least I think that's what he said. Then they defang them before the festival. Amazing! I've always found snakes fascinating—so smooth and silky and muscular."

"I told you I hated snakes. How could you do that to me?" I said, my eyes fixed on the road ahead. I couldn't bring myself to look at him.

"I figured you could handle it. Come on! You're tough!" Sander made a fist and banged it against the steering wheel. "I figured baptism by fire was a good way to confront your phobia."

"Thank you, Doctor Sander." I felt lightheaded, and my cold body, emptied of nourishment, shivered.

"The kid didn't mean any harm."

"Can we please just stop talking about it?" I wanted to gag him, to silence him in any way I could.

"Primitive, you know, like the rest of them. A bit of an asshole."

"Yeah. Asshole," I said, settling back against the headrest and pretending to nod off.

* * *

When we arrived at the hotel, I gave the welcoming mannequin a salutary wave; I was growing accustomed to her. The signora's mood had changed. The morning's vivacity gone, she appeared downcast and preoccupied as she handed us the key.

"We made it to Cocullo," Sander said.

"Ah, *si*. How did you find it?"

"Interesting, that's for sure."

"Is a curious tradition. I am glad that you go."

I wanted to blast her for having suggested the damn place, but she looked so sad and perturbed.

"*Tutto posto?*" I dared to use the phrase a waiter at my favorite Italian restaurant back home always spoke when he desired to know if all was satisfactory with his customers.

She grimaced and shrugged, then, as if grateful to have been given the opportunity, spilled out her troubles.

"Something terrible happen. The signore in the room next to you. He never come down all morning. When the maid could not get into his room to clean, we open it. He die. There, in our hotel bed. *Em-beh*," she said, raising her eyebrows and raising her palms in an eloquent *What can you do?*

"Oh my God! That's awful!" My stomach muscles constricted. I didn't dare let on about what we'd heard.

She nodded.

"Was he alone?"

"*Si*, signora. Alone. *Povero*. A pity."

Sander's silence was deafening. Once in our room he immediately drew the weighty drapes, stretched out on the bed without removing his sneakers, and, closing his eyes, claimed he wanted to nap. As far as I knew he never napped. In fact, he prided himself on not needing one. A need to repent—or forget—I assumed. Exhausted, I sank into the overstuffed armchair in a corner of the dark room and wept. It had been a disturbing day.

* * *

Apparently remorse came easily to Sander, because he woke from his nap refreshed and all smiles, eager to set out for our new favorite trattoria. I, on the other hand, had not stopped thinking about the man on the other side of the wall, but I waited until we were out of the hotel and beyond the proprietor's earshot before I broached the subject.

The restaurateur was happy to see us. He seated us at the same table we'd occupied the night before and signaled permission to help ourselves to the abundant buffet on the long table. Sander rearranged his silverware and dug in while I rearranged the food on my plate, despite the hunger pangs knotting my stomach.

"You're not eating?" Sander said after swallowing a mouthful of roasted eggplant.

"I think we have to address this, Sander."

"What?"

"The man in the room. Cocullo. The day."

"I thought you were over the snake incident. As for the man—" He put down his fork and covered my hand with his. "How could we know what was happening? You can't just react to every situation you interpret without sufficient facts. There was no way to know he was ill. It wasn't our place to intrude. We could have caused him and maybe some woman a most embarrassing situation. Maybe exposed something illicit, and who knows what the ramifications of that might have meant for their lives?"

"Jesus, Sander! You must be kidding."

"Besides, even if we had acted, it all happened so fast, we wouldn't have been able to save him."

"You don't know that. You don't know that at all."

"Don't be so naïve, lady. Grow up. And eat something. You haven't had a thing all day. You'll feel better after you do. You're a bear on an empty stomach."

He was right, at least about one thing: I *was* a bear on an empty stomach. And I was a tiger on a full one. I disengaged my hand and dug in.

The panna cotta and espresso were to die for. When the waiter brought the check, Sander asked if I wanted to get it, since we usually alternated paying.

"Do you mind covering this one?" I said. "I left my bag in the room."

"That was chancy and unlike you."

"I'm not worried. I like the signora. You can just trust some people."

He shrugged and took out his wallet. Then we strolled back to the hotel, our appetites satiated and our spirits lightened by the grappa that had topped off an exquisite meal.

Despite his nap, Sander fell asleep the moment his head hit the pillow. I couldn't be sure if it was because he was tired, inebriated, or bored with me and my behavior. It didn't really matter. Tomorrow was another day. A new dawn in Sulmona that I wouldn't be there to see. What it brought would also be left to my imagination. The snake that might or might not have been defanged, the viper that had crawled into the tote bag I zipped shut before exiting the porta potty and let loose under the sheet where Sander lay sleeping, slithering toward his naked body. A stunned Sander would wake up alone, unaware of what was happening to him. He would cry out for help. But I wouldn't hear him.

Sunrise

Marguerite woke up in anticipation of the sunrise, as she did most mornings. Her bearings were uncertain in the darkness, as uncertain, it seemed, as her situation in life. She was in the Craftsman-style house on Willow Street: bathroom on the right, hall on the left, Karl lying beside her. Or she was in the efficiency she and Karl had leased in Manhattan for a short time in their early days together while she attended design school and he navigated the world of hedge funds and municipal bonds: bathroom on the left, kitchenette on the right, Karl beside her on a secondhand waterbed that weighed heavily on the parquet of their third-story space. Sometimes she was spot-on and occupying the deteriorating nineteenth-century New England farmhouse they were renting from an absentee landlord: long narrow hallway on the right, bathroom at the end, and Karl—always Karl—lying beside her.

She stretched her left arm out toward him. They had a peculiar sleeping arrangement: at home she slept on the right side of the bed and he on the left, but when they traveled, for some reason they reversed their positions. They couldn't figure why this occurred, but it was a consensual arrangement. They hadn't ventured away from home for a long time, and, on this particularly cold February morning, she wondered if the hiatus had obviated their sleeping tradition and they'd no longer claim the opposite sides of the bed should they again find themselves in an unfamiliar environment. She reached out farther, her muscular arm bathed in the warmth of a heavy quilt, the radiators hissing, signaling the occupants to take their first steps on the splintering pine boards as they shuffled off to relieve themselves. The first riser never flushed the toilet, knowing the other was fast on his or her heels while he or she went on to brush filmy teeth and put drops in cloudy eyes.

Her hand felt around the sheet like a blind woman taking her bearings. She reluctantly opened her eyelids and brushed away the stray blond tresses that covered her left eye and cheek, but the expensive window blinds were doing their job. She knew they would; she could tell a good product from a bad one. A rooster crowed. Not their rooster; they'd never wanted to raise chickens along with water buffalo. No, it was the rooster from Chet Wojcik's dairy farm several fields away that could be heard at daybreak. Damn daybreak. That's exactly what it meant: a break—from her illusory happy state.

* * *

When the rooster crowed, Javier was already awake, having tossed and turned all night. Today was the day. As his mother had instructed, he'd told no one he was leaving San Sebastián. She wasn't really his mother but his aunt; his mother was in the US, waiting for him. But on her last phone call, she too had told him to keep silent as far as their plans were concerned.

Life was good in San Sebastián. El Salvador had finally moved beyond the era of violent political unrest; the people liked its current leader. Javier played marbles and soccer with his friends from middle school, swam in a nearby lake, enjoyed family gatherings, and occasionally—but enough—saw the father who had left his mother for another woman. Life was good. Probably better, he guessed, than the childhoods of most of the kids in the US. Had it not been for his mother—the mother who bore him—he'd never be leaving.

When Alitza and Ramón came to the door, Javier was ready with his backpack stuffed with four pairs of everything: socks, pants,

T-shirts, underwear; several bottles of water; and some *popusas*—the tortillas his aunt had made with corn flour and filled with fried beans and pork rinds because she thought they would keep better than the chicken he preferred. There was a baggie filled with *yuca frita*, deep-fried cassava bought from a street vendor, okay but not as good as when they were piping hot, and several sweet empanadas she'd made from *plátanos* and filled with beans instead of *leche*, again because she knew beans would last longer.

"*Es la hora*," his aunt whispered as she bent over the bed, her hand brushing his forehead. He pushed the covers away. He had slept in his street clothes, even his sneakers. It was time, and he was ready. Excitement to meet the mother he hadn't seen in eight years tempered the farewells—to his aunt and uncle, his friends, and his cousins Enrique, Lily, and Alina, who had been like his older siblings.

Alitza and Ramón weren't total strangers. They had come to the house one evening to discuss the plans. They were coyotes, hired by his mother to guide him and others along the dangerous route. Everyone had to do something to survive. They had not minimized the difficulty of the journey, especially for children. To some, thirteen-year-old Javier might have been considered a man. To his parents and, at this moment, to himself, he was still a child. What one has no concept of, one has no fear of.

Es la hora, Javier told himself. *Es la hora.*

"*¡Qué Dios te bendiga!*" his aunt said, putting her hand on his forehead and asking God to bless him before she turned away so he could not see her tears.

There is more to preparing for a journey like this one than arranging for food and clothing, and Javier's education had been insufficient. A certain mental preparation is also essential. Traveling in daylight is adventuresome; traveling at night is terrifying. As he would learn.

Every footstep was dangerous. Water was no longer his playmate but an obstacle to overcome. Was it a river? A lake? No matter. It was cold and teemed with slimy creatures that stung and left him itchy or in pain, and its silty bottom trapped his feet so it was hard to pull them loose.

¡Apúrate, apúrate! he was told again and again by Alitza and Ramón, often with outstretched hands. Also from the seven other Salvadoreans traveling with him: a family of three, two single men for whom this was their third attempt to reach the US, and a young husband whose wife wept a lot at night.

Hurry! Hurry! Always hurry at night. Always creep slowly by day. He had already run out of water and his empty bottle was filled from Alitza's until they could safely stop somewhere to buy more. He had run out of food, too. Several times the coyotes bought them *yuca frita* and *tamal pisque* from street vendors, and on one occasion a turkey sandwich and sweet *horchata* to drink. Still, he was hungry much of the time. He was tired and cold when they emerged from the water and set foot in Guatemala. And he was lonely. He tried to stave off fear with thoughts of the mother who had left him, the mother he had learned to live without.

A car with a trailer was waiting for them in Guatemala. At first Javier thought that now things would be easier than the days on foot, but he was mistaken. Crouching under a small table and unable to lie down most of the way, others covered with a tarp, it was difficult to breathe the smell of soured cheese and frying grease that lingered on their breaths and mingled with the body odors that accumulated with no access to soap and water. Javier was sore when Ramón gingerly unfolded his skinny arms and legs and, as though he were the most delicate moth whose wings might disintegrate, pulled him out of the trailer.

"*¿Estamos en los Estados Unidos?*" Javier asked.

"No, *chico. Estamos en Monterrey. En México.*"

They stayed four days on a crowded Monterrey Street, in the house they had entered by way of a dark alley. Someone's house. Someone who prepared tortillas and fried eggs that they ate from plastic plates on the living room floor, where they remained for three nights and days. And there was fruit, and water, and a bathroom with a sink and toilet where they were allowed to hand wash and relieve themselves. Javier brushed his teeth for the first time during his journey, hesitating before spitting out the rinse water, as he was accustomed to doing, not wanting to waste what had become precious.

There wasn't much conversation among the travelers, as one would tell another to stay quiet. Always to remain quiet. Especially the young bride, whimpering in her husband's arms as he soothed her with murmurs that Javier guessed were of adoration and plans for their future across the border.

He never saw Aliza and Ramón after they were dropped off at the house, or the woman of the house who stayed in the kitchen or bedroom, her and her husband's voices drowned out by the voices coming from a television. If the man left, it was through the back door they had all come in through. He never passed through the crowded living room, with its thin, stained carpeting, except to bring their one meal each day or a second mug of coffee in the afternoon. After several days—Javier had lost count, perhaps three or four—the man in his worn jeans, checkered flannel shirt, and a wide belt buckle handed a bottle of water and a bus pass to each of them and directed them to walk to the bus station to catch the evening coach destined for the border. But when they arrived, they were put on another bus by Mexican immigration and sent back to El Salvador.

"It is possible to make the journey," the bus driver who took over in Guatemala said. "I lived and worked in the US for ten years. Then I got deported by ICE. I'm happy to be back in Guatemala, no matter what. Here, despite my poverty and dangerous conditions, I have my family. My compatriots. My dignity. *Mi dignidad.* I would rather hard labor in a slum than face the humiliation of deportation again." He wished them luck.

Happy to see his family again, to be once more in the warm safety of home, Javier was at the same time disappointed that his effort had failed through no fault of his own. What would he tell his mother? The mother who had made it to the US alone eight years earlier, who had said, "I love you, and I'll be back." It had been the third time she had left for the US, and after several months of washing dishes in a Mexican restaurant, she had always returned. But that last time he knew from her voice that something was off. He was only seven, yet he knew that time would be different.

He had no time to nurse his disappointment: two weeks later he was woken before sunrise to find Alitza and Ramón ready to begin another journey. Only this time Javier would not be alone: his older cousin Mañuel and his wife Elena would go with him. His aunt cried twice as hard this time. "*¡Que Dios los bendiga!*" she said, her hand going from one forehead to the other.

* * *

Marguerite was a Southern California girl who had fallen hard for the olive-skinned Karl Siracconi. And while short family lifespans had robbed him of relatives to return to, his hometown tugged at him. Or was it the fact that he could never worm his way into the big-time houses like Morgan Stanley and Goldman Sachs the way most of his fellow alumni had? Marguerite never knew which was his Achilles' heel: the tug from home that sabotaged his career or the subpar performance that made him yearn for home during his years at a small investment firm. Whichever it was, she was okay with moving to western Massachusetts. Karl could talk her into almost anything—even raising European water buffalo and going into the mozzarella business. After nearly thirty years in the foot-hills of the Berkshires, she had grown accustomed to the cold gray of winter, the icy grip of snow and the hibernation it allowed, the crackling of a roaring fire, the smell of maple sap boiling in a sugar shack, the smoke from a wood-burning stove. She had grown to appreciate—even love—the changing seasons that never made her tire of the lovely landscape.

But that was then, and this was now. Time to rise. There was always work to be done on a dairy farm regardless of the season, independent of the volume or number of products, and despite extenuating circumstances. Miss Penelope, whose toffee, black, and white fur seemed to have grown duller and grayer the past year, knew that. Stress, Marguerite concluded. Stress, the veterinarian confirmed. Marguerite's golden hair, which had never darkened, now began to show signs of white—or, as she termed it, platinum. Miss Penelope jumped onto the quilt and burrowed beneath it. It's time, she purred, nudging her mistress. It's time.

* * *

The second time around for Javier would be somewhat different— shorter. The fellow travelers also different: two middle-aged laborers from San Salvador, two men about Mañuel's age from Honduras. And they talked more, despite Aliza's and Ramón's warnings, the older men telling tales of the ones they knew who had made it— like Javier's mother—who were now working and living in nice homes and sending money back to their families, but also of those, like themselves, who had been sent back by the US government.

"A man from my town had been in the US for over twenty years, with a wife and three children, when ICE picked him up for failing to pay outstanding parking tickets years before," one of the younger men said. "He managed to get sanctuary in a church. He has been there for three years while his family and community advocates plead for his stay."

"ICE put me in solitary confinement for forty-five days!" an older man said. "They put people behind bars just for wanting a better life. ICE should be done away with."

"¿Por qué?" Mañuel asked earnestly as they lay again on the soiled rug in the house in Monterrey, but this time for only one night. "Why do you want to cross the border again?"

"For the ability to speak my mind. To go out and protest. To advocate for human rights. For the others. That, to me, is freedom."

"I have a son," the older man said. "I brought him across the border when he was only three years old. I got a job washing dishes in an Italian restaurant. Then I learned to cook—pizza, pasta, every-thing they served. They paid me under the table, as they say. My wife cleaned houses. I bought a house. They gave me a mortgage. I had nice furniture. But when my mother was dying, I foolishly went back to Honduras and left my son with his mother. Now I can't get back. The United States is all my son knows. Springfield, Illinois, is all he knows. Under Obama he had DACA status—he could stay so long as he kept out of trouble—but Trump has taken it away," he said, with a swift motion of his hand. "And my son lives in fear."

"He's what they call a Dreamer, no?" Mañuel asked.

"*Sí*. He is a Dreamer."

"In life we are all dreamers," the other man said.

At nightfall, the man of the house drove them to the border as he was supposed to have done the first time. But before they left, he gave Javier a piece of paper with a telephone number written in blue ink. "*Míralo hasta que lo sepas por memoria*," he instructed Javier, so the boy memorized it before the man took it back and ripped it up. Seven minutes was all it took to get to the Rio Grande. The river was calm that day as they all squeezed into a boat large enough for three adults. Once they reached the other side, someone started yelling directions to go here or there. And to hurry. Always hurry.

After having traveled the last three days on foot and with no sleep the night before, Javier was dizzy and unsure of what he was seeing as the group made their way up the riverbank: the wall of steel and two men dressed in the same drab green of the rug in the house in Monterrey. The men wore sunglasses, matching baseball caps, and wide belts holding flashlights and radios and guns. It was easy to guess what was written in large yellow letters across the backs of their shirts and on the badges on their sleeves. They were Border Patrol: one Latino looking, the other Anglo and eating soup out of a paper container with a plastic spoon. He put the spoon back in the container and offered it to Javier.

"*Toma. Está bien*," the Latino officer assured him.

"*Está cansado*," the agent with the soup said in poorly accented Spanish. He seemed to recognize Javier's fatigue. "*¿No tiene hambre?*"

He took the soup. Yes, he was tired and hungry—very hungry. It was hot chicken soup, with carrots and celery and rice, much like the kind his aunt made, that slid down to his empty stomach faster than hard rain down a drainpipe. And it was good.

* * *

Just rip the Band-Aid off, honey, Marguerite heard Karl say. That's what he always said about tackling daunting tasks. And so, at 5:15 every morning, she got up, shuffled down the long narrow hall to the bathroom, and relieved herself while she brushed her teeth. She was a good multitasker. She combed her hair with her fingers and twisted it up into a bun she secured with a fat tortoiseshell clip, unintentionally leaving some stragglers to frame her windburned, freckled face. In her youth, men had found her attractive in a surfer girl way. But she was now in her mid-fifties, and after having worked six years on a dairy farm—the last one alone—admirers had gone as far as to describe her all-American beauty as "rustic femininity." *That was putting it kindly*, she thought.

"You need to trim your bangs," she told her image in the mirror of the antique medicine cabinet that didn't close properly due to countless layers of white enamel paint. The long fringe of platinum hair had begun to mingle with her lashes and hinder her vision, but she didn't have time to fuss over her appearance. Karl used to say that makeup made her look like some painted showgirl in a Toulouse-Lautrec poster and that she should let her natural good looks speak for themselves. She was down with that. One less thing to do. Females worked way too hard trying to improve their physical features or hold off the aging process for the sake of males who never spent more than five minutes on their appearance. She vowed that in her next life she was coming back as a man; until then she'd be grateful that an *au naturel* look suited her and her loved one just fine.

Even when Karl was in the hospital undergoing cancer treatment and Marguerite had given up her interior design business, she strapped on her boots and rubber pants each day and ran the dairy and creamery alone, with Karl on speakerphone talking her through the new challenges she was facing. After three months the cancer seemed to have disappeared; Karl came home, and life was better than good again. But a month later, tests showed that it had spread from his pancreas to his back and spine. She'd pulled the Band-Aid off then for a different reason: she shut down the dairy operation to be at Karl's side and see him through to the end of his life's journey. A month later she was back sweeping away spilled buffalo milk and hay from her barn floor, handling the milking, and forming shimmering, porcelain-white, fist-sized spheres of mozzarella that she delivered to her high-end restaurant customers every Thursday and Sunday. She never seemed to stop moving, as if afraid that if she did, even to catch her breath for a moment, her world would come tumbling down around her.

* * *

Javier wasn't sure where the border patrolmen took them in their large white SUVs. It was a big city—maybe El Paso—with lots of lights and large buildings with gates. When they reached the first gate, they met others who'd also been brought by patrolmen. There, they separated the adults from the children and teenagers, then the girls from the boys. Suddenly Mañuel and Elena were gone, and Javier found himself in a large cell-like room with several other boys. They were given big sheets of silver paper to unfold and use as blankets that didn't keep them warm, and sandwiches and apples. Javier should have been frightened, but he wasn't. He had made it across the border, and the people he had encountered were kind.

Javier made friends—he always made friends—with a boy from Guatemala and another from Honduras while he was held at the border. They fashioned hats and airplanes and animal figures out of the silver paper blankets. He never saw Mañuel or Elena. He did, however, get to talk to his mother on the one phone call he was allowed during his stay, and he knew what number to call: the one the man who owned the house in Monterrey had given him to memorize. Her voice was so high-pitched with excitement when he told her he'd made it across the border and that he was fine—he was good—that he could barely understand what she said next.

"Listen," she told him. "Do what they tell you, *hijito mío*. Stay out of trouble and away from troublemakers. It won't be much longer."

The next day he and his new friends José and Ricardo were given forms to fill out and orange jumpsuits to change into. His was short and he didn't like that his bony ankles showed between the hem of the pants and his filthy and torn sneakers. It never occurred to him that they might be headed to prison although it should have, because that's how convicts were dressed in movies. They were driven to the airport and put on a plane that, a few hours later, landed in New York City, where they were met by a dark-skinned man in a navy-blue sweatsuit who introduced himself as Mr. Robertson.

It was a relatively short drive to a sprawling two-story mansion with white columns in the country. The boys couldn't believe they were still in New York; they marveled at the trees and rolling green hills that stretched as far as they could see. Now Javier understood. This was the America everyone risked their lives to get to. This was paradise.

As luck would have it, he was shown to a bedroom he would share with another boy from El Salvador. In the dresser he found several outfits that included everything from underwear to a new pair of sneakers. A little black case on the dresser held a new toothbrush and toothpaste, soap, shampoo, and a comb. When it was dinnertime and Javier and his roommate, along with José and Ricardo and their roommates, filed into the dining hall to sit at long tables already set for them, a lot of boys came over to introduce themselves. Most were from Honduras, or Guatemala, or El Salvador, and a few from Mexico. Many were his age, and some three or four years older. But they weren't all refugees who had been separated from their parents in their attempt to enter the US. There were American boys at this place called Lincoln Hall, too, boys who were there because of some bad thing they had done, but most of them were nice to Javier and his friends, shaking hands with them, telling them which dishes were better than others, and pointing out the way to the bathrooms, the gymnasium, the library, the outdoor tennis and basketball courts—so many basketball courts.

Javier met lots of good people at Lincoln Hall. He had been born with a calm demeanor, an abundance of patience, and an ability to adapt and make the best of a situation even at a young age. He had been raised in a safe and loving family, but he knew that that was not the case for all the boys his age in El Salvador, and for some—like Trey—at Lincoln Hall. But if he kept a cool head and posed no threat, he was almost always able to turn a difficult situation around.

English lessons started after lunch on the day of Javier's arrival. The boys got to choose between cooking in the big kitchen or playing sports as their extracurricular activity; Javier opted to play soccer during his month's stay and was assigned a gym locker but no lock, since the boys were on the honor system at Lincoln Hall. The South American boys always held an advantage over their American counterparts, soccer having been their only sporting outlet from the time they were able to walk, and Javier's agility, speed, and superiority at ball handling and maintaining possession embarrassed his defenders—especially Trey—during their first scrimmage.

On his second day Javier's shin guards went missing, but since South Americans never wore shin guards because they played a highly technical and refined game, Javier took to the field without them, aware that the highly physical American style often led to dirty play. This time a frustrated Trey did indeed take the dirty route to clear out the immigrant the next time he was faced with defending him. He swung through so wide and strong on the kick that even when Trey didn't get the ball he upended Javier, a foul that left Javier lying on the ground with a fresh wound on his shin. Only after repeated takedowns did the physical education teacher stop the play and inspect Javier for injuries. When he questioned his lack of shin guards beneath his long socks, Javier raised his palms, assuming full responsibility although he knew Trey must have taken them. The next day the guards reappeared in his cubby; that evening Trey approached Javier's table at dinner, asking if he could join him and his friends. In time Lincoln Hall became another home for Javier, where the food was good, and where, as always, he made lots of friends. He really loved it.

On his fourteenth birthday, when the leaves on the trees had begun to turn yellow and red, and the air became chilly, Mr. Robertson took Javier aside. He was smiling, saying that something was going to happen to him. Javier's English was still not good enough to understand most of what Mr. Robertson was saying, and rather than admit that or offend his mentor, he just kept nodding, saying, "Oh, yeah? Good! Great!" Later that day, Mr. Robertson took Javier to the director's office, where he immediately recognized one of the two smiling women: the woman in the photos sent him over the years, to whom he'd been speaking once or twice a week during his time at Lincoln Hall. It seemed she had given no indication she'd be coming so soon so as not to disappoint him should she be held up. It was crazy. It was joyous. He ran into her open arms and prepared for yet another separation from new friends, from a new home.

He said goodbye to Ricardo and José, to his roommate and the other boys, and got into the car driven by the other woman, who was his mother's friend. Then he waved at the boys as it pulled out of the driveway.

"You can stay in touch with them," his mother said. And he believed her. She had never lied to him.

* * *

"Would you like some coffee? Frost on the pumpkin this morning," Marguerite said, looking up at her neighbor Chet, who had stepped into her milking barn at an hour when most people were just rising. "I'm pretty much finished here. I know you can't resist my latte." She smiled, disconnected the tubes from Adele's udder, and wiped her teats with a washcloth before she patted the buffalo.

After cleaning her hands with another cloth, she walked over to the espresso machine perched on the splintering timber that served as a coffee bar.

"More than frost. Hell, it's ten degrees. So much for a January thaw. Besides, Marguerite, you know I'm a sucker for your buffalo milk latte. I hate to admit it's a tad better than the milk my Holsteins produce. I've already had the two-cup limit my cardiologist prescribed, but what the hell, we've both got a long day ahead of us."

"Unlike you, I only have to milk once a day," she said.

"And unlike you, I got my son and two part-time helpers."

When the espresso machine sputtered, signaling that its final drop of foam had dropped into the rich black coffee, Marguerite brought a mug over to Chet, who'd taken a seat on a hay bale. His round head with its blue woolen cap and weathered cheeks resembled a cue ball; the skin on his face and hands—and on the rest of his sturdy frame, she imagined—was smooth and plump despite his age, as though it had been botoxed.

"You actually sit?" Marguerite said, teasing.

"On occasion. More and more these days. You're the one to talk."

Gladys Knight sauntered up to Marguerite and nudged her for some of the affection she'd shown Adele. She petted the black silky hair between the cow's elegantly curved horns and then told her to go over to her offspring and the other ladies. "Bonding time," she said, which was, according to her, the secret of generous milk flow. "Happy wife, milky life."

"I didn't know they married," Chet said.

"Poetic license. Couldn't find another word to rhyme. Maybe 'Easy goes, more milk flows.'"

Chet pursed his lips, as if to say, "Really, Marguerite?"

"Okay. Maybe not. But you know the deal: The happier they are, the more they're loved, the more they produce."

"I know," Chet said, nodding. There was no need to explain herself: providing a loving environment for the cows was clearly a valid concept.

"I'm thinking you didn't come for a cup of coffee, and you mended that hole in the fence a few days ago, so what's up, my friend?" she asked as she hefted the heavy pail of fresh milk onto the hook of a hanging scale. Satisfied with the weight, she poured the milk into a large funnel atop a stainless steel vat, covered the vat with its lid, took a broom from a corner of the stall, and began sweeping the milking area. "Checking up on me?"

"Is that a bad thing, Marguerite? You know, in the year Karl's been gone, I don't think I've seen you stand still once. You sleeping at night?"

"Are you?" She knew there were dark circles under her eyes; she couldn't remember the last time she'd worn makeup. She looked down at her fingers—each one red from the cold, the cuticles dry and cracked, the nails brittle and torn.

"I'm older than you. Everyone my age has sleeping issues," Chet said.

"And women my age do, too."

"*Touché*, Marguerite. But you know what I'm getting at. You could use some help. And with more calves due by spring—"

She took a deep breath and turned away from him as her eyes welled up. She hated when this happened in front of anyone. Of course, she needed help. He was spot-on. She squeezed the broomstick hard. Why was it so difficult to admit her vulnerability? Since Karl died, she found herself counting every step she took on the hall stairs to fill the time it took to get from one floor to another. She avoided looking at the clock, dreading that empty hour in the day when she was alone and bored. Even short car rides seemed long now. Time moved too slowly while she waited for night and the chance to dream of being with Karl. There was nothing unusual about any of this. She was nobody special, she told herself. Just one more human being who could no longer listen to music that now triggered the pain of loss, one more human being who missed her mate so very damn much.

"Marguerite, you're one of the strongest women I know. Just like my LuAnn was. But even she knew, as much as she hated to admit it, when it was time to ask for help. Only she got around it by giving orders. But we all knew it meant the last straw was about to land on that mighty camel."

"My, my, Chet. You should have been a shrink," Marguerite said, wiping a tear from her cheek before she turned to face him.

"Too much indoor schooling. I need to be outdoors—like Karl," he told her.

"Help is hard to come by nowadays. Especially reliable help. Got any ideas?"

"I do," he replied.

* * *

"Can you jump that fence?" Marguerite asked Javier. "It's not electrified. And please don't step on Miss Penelope if she gets in your way." She pointed to the cat at her feet who was curiously taking in the skinny boy.

Javier looked at the wire strands strung between metal posts and back at Marguerite with a puzzled expression.

"Sometimes a buffalo—usually one of the studs—can break out and chase you, and you've got nowhere to go but over another one—fence, that is."

He took a few steps backward and made a run for the fence the way he had learned to do when he jumped over hurdles at Lincoln Hall or rows of rubber tires in San Sebastián. Landing safely on the other side, although on the ground, he looked up at her, waiting to see if he had passed her test.

"Nice!" she said, congratulating him.

After that day and his first encounter with Marguerite, who insisted he call her by her first name, he came to the farm three mornings a week before school, before daylight, walking a mile in the dark from the apartment he shared with his mother and cousins in a low-income complex. Marguerite had offered to pick him up, but he knew she hated to waste the time required to finish her chores, and his mother needed the few extra hours of sleep before she started her seemingly endless workday in the city. Besides, he felt most at peace walking in the dark: the once scary blackness now offered a feeling of safety and invisibility. When he finished working, Marguerite drove him to the school bus stop and waited in her car, despite his protests, until he was on board. Even when he put in time after school or on weekends helping Marguerite with guided tours of the farm, when children and their families could pet the buffalo, sample mozzarella made that morning, and picnic on tables set up next to the huts, Javier waited until twilight, chatting with Marguerite about the animals or the new book he was reading in English class, before heading home.

He had been in the States for a year now, having spent six months in middle school mostly taking ESL classes. When his command of English improved, he was sent on to the regional high school, where he had fallen in with a fellow classmate whose grand-father, or Jaja Chet, as the boy called him, owned a dairy farm. He was a kind man, like so many of the people he had met, and when he asked Javier if he'd like to work for Marguerite, Javier jumped at the chance. Where in El Salvador would he have been paid for working at his age? Most grown-ups couldn't find employment.

Marguerite said she couldn't afford to pay Javier as much as she'd have liked, but it was more than enough. His mother no lon-ger had to give her son spending money or cash for school supplies. She worked three jobs to pay the rent for the two-bedroom apart-ment they shared with Mañuel and Elena—who also worked long hours at a different restaurant in the nearest city—and to buy food and clothing. Another reason Javier liked hanging out at the farm was that reminded him of the attractive landscape and privacy he'd enjoyed at Lincoln Hall. He also missed the camaraderie at the school and in his home in San Sebastián. As much as he loved his mother and his cousins, their desire to survive in the US meant that they were hardly ever at home, and when they were, they needed sleep.

Chet wanted to see this smart, earnest boy succeed, and, above all, not fall into bad company. Keeping busy was the best way to avoid it, and it was the logic behind the work ethic he instilled in his own children. Furthermore, he knew that Marguerite would teach Javier more than how to milk a cow and clean a stall. She was intelligent. She would talk to him, and he would hear good English spoken and help him with his homework. And while he knew she struggled to keep the dairy farm in business, he assumed she might have connections through college alumni and wealthy clients to lawyers and politicians who might come in handy for Javier one day. Most important, Marguerite had a good heart: anyone who could cuddle with a water buffalo and design a bovine nursery that rivaled a state-of-the-art human birthing facility could open her heart to a boy who didn't think he was in need but who, Chet knew, was. As was she. A no-brainer, Chet thought. A win-win situation.

* * *

Javier was in the pasteurization shed that autumn day, almost three years to the date when he had left Lincoln Hall, as he watched Marguerite about to dip her hands into the cauldron of prepared milk that had become stringy and rubbery and start squeezing out the luscious, glistening white balls of cheese—a process that never failed to delight the teen. Today the proceedings were interrupted by Miss Penelope's drawn-out wailing from outside the shed. After discovering that the cat's distress was caused by a drama taking place nearby, Javier ran back in to tell Marguerite that Lady Gaga and what he thought was her new calf were stuck in a metal fence.

"We could break the fence apart," Marguerite said, quickly weighing her options. "I saw Karl do it once, but I've never done it by myself."

She ripped off her cheesemaker's white jacket and hat, letting her hair fly every which way as she shed her boots and marched toward the barn. There she put on a muddy old pair and dumped oats from a massive feed bag into a plastic bin. As she made a beeline for the trapped buffalo, Javier followed at her heels. Gently rubbing

Lady Gaga's shoulders, she guided her chunky head to the snack. A few gentle maneuvers later and the cow's head, with its massive curled horns, had been freed. Marguerite repeated the maneuver with the calf, and soon Marguerite herself was also free—to return to the milking shed and her work.

Feats like this amazed Javier. If he was learning anything from Marguerite, it wasn't how to hook up a milking machine, or birth a calf, or conduct a petting zoo tour, or even interpret Homer's *Odyssey*. It was the conviction that there was always a way to solve a problem. A person just had to be creative and find the one that worked, the one that could even resolve a situation that seemed doomed to fail.

* * *

Javier was nearing the end of his junior year in high school when the ground beneath him shifted. He and Marguerite had begun talking about the colleges he might apply to in the fall. She had taken him to speak to an admissions director at a prestigious local school that was looking to diversify and was willing to provide scholarships to those in need who had outlined a goal they hoped to achieve. Mañuel and Elena had moved into their own apartment in the city and were expecting a baby, and Javier was able to abandon the couch and move into their former bedroom in the apartment he shared with his mother, who was working harder than ever. Life was—he was cautiously optimistic—good. That is, until the day Javier got a call from Mañuel on his new cell phone, telling him not to go home after school, not to get off at the bus stop near the apartment, but to go the farm and stay there. Things were no longer good.

ICE. They must have worked hard to arrive at such a cold and heartless acronym, he thought. What do you do when you run into ice? Chop away at it? Only if you have the right tools. Tread gingerly? Only if it's a thin glaze. Wait patiently—doing everything in your power to keep warm and avoid frostbite—for it to melt and become passable? Only if the temperature looks like it'll rise. For an immigrant without a visa, what can they do? Ice had taken down the *Titanic*, hadn't it?

He had read Eugene O'Neill's *The Iceman Cometh* in English class, a play about men unable to go on once they were forced to confront the illusions they harbored about their lives. Is that what the desire for a better life was? An illusion? Now his mother was being detained in a prison. The ICE men had come.

She had refused to answer questions posed by the three officers dressed as local police who approached her as she stepped off the bus on her way to work that morning. She had said she wanted to speak to a lawyer. But she had also not made a scene and walked away with them so she wouldn't look guilty, and in so doing she had unknowingly surrendered to them. It was too late to run to a church and ask for sanctuary. Within forty-eight hours, she would be on a plane back to El Salvador.

There had been a complaint about stealing by a former employer whose advances she had rejected. They had been following her. It isn't easy to live in America without papers. Her tourist visa had expired years ago, and frightened and ignorant of the legalities, she hadn't sought a stay-of-removal order. She had simply tried to stay under the radar. Mind her own business. Live in the shadows.

* * *

Marguerite woke up in anticipation of the sunrise, before the rooster crowed, as she did most mornings, moving uncertainly in the dark. She stretched her left arm out toward Karl, and, feeling the emptiness, withdrew it. That was then and this was now. She pushed off the quilt and, her bare feet silent on the wide pine boards, headed down the hall to the small bedroom on the right and knocked on the door.

"It's time," she said.

"*Sí,*" the boy mumbled, momentarily confused by his surroundings as he woke from his dream. "*Es la hora.*"

Acknowledgments

As always I am indebted to the "Canadian Connection": my friend and editor Chris Jerome, and to Jennifer Dinsmore, and especially to the marvelous Michael Mirolla and everyone at Guernica Editions who believe that literature, culture, and publishing know no boundaries.

Fiction does not appear out of thin air. Even stories believed to have sprung purely out of one's imagination, consciously or subconsciously, have threads of reality woven into their fabrics. And then there is the intentional gathering of information provided by those who have graciously offered their time, expertise, and experience. Heartfelt thanks to: Henrry Aguiluz, Brendan Baker, Brian Confalone, Gordy Cook, the late Anthony Licata, and Jean Ruggiero. A special nod to my faithful and careful readers Susan Harris, Betsy Hartmann, and Joann Kobin. To the late Shirley and John Piniat for the cover sketch I discovered among their copious artwork. And to the man who walks not only in my dreams but thankfully in every day of my life, my husband Martin Wohl.

About the Author

Marisa Labozzetta is the author of three novels and two previous works of short fiction. She is a three-time Eric Hoffer Award winner, a Pushcart Prize nominee, and a Binghamton University John Gardner Fiction Award Finalist. Her short stories have received the Watchung Arts Festival and the Rio Grande Writers First Prizes, and honorable mention for Playboy's Victoria Chen-Haider Memorial Award. Her work has appeared in *The American Voice, Beliefnet.com, The Florida Review, VIA, Italian Americana, The Penguin Book of Italian American Writing, Show Me A Hero: Great Contemporary Stories about Sports, Celebrating Writers of the Pioneer Valley, KnitLit,* and the bestselling *When I Am an Old Woman I Shall Wear Purple,* among other publications. Her novel, *A Day in June,* received the Eric Hoffer Grand Prize Short List Award and American Best Book Award 2020, and Best New Fiction Award Finalist and American Fiction Book Award 2019. "The Woman Who Drew on Walls," from this collection, was a New Millennium Fiction Award Finalist. Marisa Labozzetta shares time between Northampton and Eastham, Massachusetts.

**For Questions and Topics for Discussion
and to contact Marisa Labozzetta visit:
www.marisalabozzetta.com.**